Thomas Pownall, John Whitaker

An Antiquarian Romance

Thomas Pownall, John Whitaker

An Antiquarian Romance

ISBN/EAN: 9783337347154

Printed in Europe, USA, Canada, Australia, Japan

Cover: Foto ©Andreas Hilbeck / pixelio.de

More available books at **www.hansebooks.com**

AN

ANTIQUARIAN ROMANCE,

ENDEAVOURING

TO MARK A LINE,

BY WHICH

THE MOST ANCIENT PEOPLE,

AND

THE PROCESSIONS OF THE EARLIEST INHABITANCY OF EUROPE,

MAY BE INVESTIGATED.

SOME REMARKS ON
Mr. WHITAKER'S CRITICISMS
ANNEXED.

By GOVERNOR POWNALL.

" Il-y-a peu de fables, qui ne foient conçues dans la
vérité même : comme il-y-a peu de vérités anciennes,
que la fable n'ait taché d'infecter et de corrompre.
Chorier, Hift. de Dauphiné."

L O N D O N:
PRINTED BY AND FOR JOHN NICHOLS.
M.DCC.XCV.

P R E F A C E.

IT may feem ſtrange, after having publiſhed a treatiſe on the
uſe of *Antiquarian* learning, marking the line, in which it ought to
be purſued, as a *commentary to
hiſtory*, that the firſt uſe I ſhould
make of it is the writing and pub-
liſhing a Romance.

What is now publiſhed was
written and finiſhed eleven years
ago, as a ſecond part to what I

then

then publifhed in 1782. I annexed, at the end of that publica-
tion, an analyfis of the contents of
this; as a fort of fyllabus that has
not been without its ufe.

Some ingenious things have
been written concerning the Picts
and Celts, and publifhed fince that
period. When the learned Antiquary compares thofe things with
the analyfis here referred to, as
publifhed fo long ago, and with
the treatife itfelf now publifhed,
he will fee that they do not, in
the leaft, interfere with thofe matters of literature, or thofe points
of information, which this treatife contains; and whence it
may affume any merit of origin-
ality.

The title of *Romance* need not
ftagger the reader's faith; for, all
hiftory

hiſtory might equally have the ſame title given to it, in thoſe parts, where it aſſumes to go back to, and to ſtate, the origin and firſt ages of nations.

I have ſaid, in the firſt part, that the diſperſed and broken fragments of any ruined pieces of architecture may be ſo put together, by a perſon ſkilled in the ſcience, as to reſtore the building in ſome degree to its original form ; and, even where many parts are loſt, yet ſo as to aſcertain what the building was. As of architecture, ſo in hiſtory ; for, the nature of men has its proportions and orders. I believe that the fact coincides with this poſition in moſt hiſtories now extant, Grecian, Roman, and Barbarian. They are a patch-work of ſcattered fragments of facts, put together ac

a 4   cording

cording to thefe proportions and órders.

This *Rómance*, therefore, founded in what are commonly confidered as facts; conducted in its edifice according to the order of the human being, in its proceffions and actions; compofed, as to its parts, of fragments and remnants of a fyftem, which once had actual exiftence, but of which the fragments now lie fcattered and neglected, partly buried in oblivion, and partly fmothered and over-grown with the weeds of fable, is, to all intents, ufe, and application, of the antient hiftory of people and nations, equally hiftory; and ftands on the fame ground and level with what the Greeks have written, as hiftory, of the origin of nations; of the Medes, Perfians, Affyrians, Ægyptians, and

of

of themfelves : on the fame ground
and level with what the Romans
have written of their Trojan origin, of the origin of the Cartha-
genians, and the nations which
they became acquainted with by
their wars : on the fame ground
and level with the fables which
the Northern European nations
have adopted, as their origin, from
Trojans, Phœnicians, and Perfians.

It is equally as good hiftory as
thefe, this difference only excepted, that it doth not demand
the readers belief, but profeffeth
itfelf to be a Romance. In this
fhape, however, it may not be
without its ufe. Some men will
pick out truths from a Romance,
or at leaft from what is fo called,
rather than from hiftory. Thofe
facts, which are offered to them
as hiftory, they will difpute and
reject ;

reject; whereas truths, which
come forward veiled in the fable
of Romance, will, whilft they in-
dulge the flattering pride of un-
veiling them, fteal upon their belief. Truths which lie thus concealed from the common eye, lie
like the rough ore in the mine,
which the ftudent, by an exertion
of his ingenuity, can elicit, refine,
and bring to light, on the face
of the learned world, as bullion,
the fruits of his own difcovery.

In reading thofe narratives which
profefs to be hiftory, the reader is
called upon to proceed with fuf-
picious caution; to have conftant
and repeated reference to what he
knows, or ought to know, of fuch
matters and things as are fuppofed
to be decided facts; to what is,
and what is not, in the actual
courfe

courfe of nature, and of man's being; in fhort, fo to read as almoft
to deftroy all pleafure in reading.
If he doth not ftudy hiftory in this
manner, he may as well, *laxa cer-
vice,* read a Romance : and this
Romance, to fuch readers, will be
full as good as hiftory.

In this treatife the facts are collected; are brought into approximation ; and, by a kind of experiment, endeavoured to be fitted
in a certain order and combination
with each other. The Romance
is only the *bead-roll* on which they
are ftrung.

If the critic is difpofed to give
credit to the narrative, he will receive the more amufement in the
reading, as the author did in the
writing, when and where he pur-
fuaded himfelf to believe it. If
he

he is not so disposed, and with-
holds not only his credit from the
narrative, but his approbation from
the literature, which is made the
foundation of it; and will not ad-
mit the facts, *quæ neque confirmare*
argumentis nec repellere in animo est *,
I shall not dispute the point with
him : I shall enter into no contro-
versy about it, nor any defence
of it, *conjecturæ in multis locum de-*
derimus, in aliis nobis ipsis vix satis-
fecerimus, conatum in medio relinquen-
tes, quô meliora et certiora docenti-
bus suus quoque esset honos et gloria †.
The very bringing the facts together, in this manner, may suggest
to his superior ingenuity some
better manner of treating them,
which may be intirely his own.
He may thus have all the credit,
which the writer of this, in all

* Tacitus.　　† Olaus Wormius.

4　　　　　　　　hu-

humility, is willing to concede to him : for thus the purpofes of knowledge may be truely ferved, whoever has the credit of the learning.

To be ferious, I am really of opinion that if the ftudy of antiquities, in thefe parts refpecting the origin and firft ages of nations, be purfued in this line of experimental inductive theorems, which do not pretend to have found out truth, but are only fearching their way to it ; learning would become more productive of real knowledge.

I fhall finifh this preface with the opinion of Monf. Chorier, as, at the fame time that it expreffes, better than I can do, the fentiment, it confirms it with his authority.—"Il eft certain, qu' il-y-a

peu

peu de fables, qui ne foient conçues dans la vérité même; comme
il-y-a peu de vérités anciennes,
que la fable n'ait taché d'infecter
et de corrompre."

EVERTON-HOUSE,
Nov. 1, 1793.

BOOKS AND TRACTS WRITTEN BY GOVERNOR POWNALL.

Adminiftration of the Britifh Colonies. 2 vols. 8vo. Cadell.

Three Memorials. 1. addreffed to the Sovereigns of Europe. 2. to the Sovereign of Great Britain. 3. to the Sovereigns of North America. Cadell.

Topographical Defcription of the Middle Colonies in North America; with a Map. Folio.

Letter from Governor Pownall to Adam Smith, LL. D. F. R. S.

Treatife on the Study of Antiquities. 8vo. Dodfley.

TRACTS.

The Rights, Interefts, and Duty of Government, as concerned in the Affairs of the Eaft Indies. 8vo. Almon, 1781.

Treatife on the hoftile Rivalfhips between the Manufacturer and Landworker, with a more fpecial View to the Conteft between the Woolen Manufacturers and Wool Growers. 8vo. Debrett, 1787.

Hydraulic and Nautical Obfervations on the Currents in the Atlantic Ocean; with a Map. Notes by Dr. Franklin. 4to. Rob. Sayer.

Memoir, entitled, Drainage and Navigation but one united Work: and an Outfall to deep Water the firft and neceffary Step to it. 8vo. Almon, 1777.

Notices and Defcriptions of Antiquities in the Provincia Romana of Gaul, &c. with an Appendix defcribing the Roman Baths and Thermæ difcovered in 1787 at Badenweiler. 4to. Nichols, 1787.

A N

ANTIQUARIAN ROMANCE.

OUR obfervations on the ftudy of Antiquities, as a commentary to hiftory, now pafs from that period (of which Antient Hiftory, as it is called, gives the narrative) to a fucceeding period, wherein a new race of men* coming up from the remote *feas*, and forth from the *forefts*, invaded the *cultured world*, and deftroyed its civilization.

The fpirit and character of thefe two periods were as different as the race of men who compofed the inhabitancy of them. The former were a race of *land-*

---

* Formæ hominum inufitatæ. T. Livius?
Animi Ferarum, corpora plufquam humana.
L. Florus, Lib. 2. cap. 4.
Jornandus, Lib. 1. § 21.

B *workers,*

workers, having permanent fettlements, and, by the procefs of community, organizing into *civil* fociety. The latter, in the firft ftages of their inhabitancy, occupied the earth in its original uncultured ftate : were rovers in the forefts, and on the feas : had no community but in their family or hord : knew no fociety but that of their hunting or predatory parties : acknowledged no government or command but what arofe of courfe out of the neceffity of concentered operation, and unity of action, in thefe excurfions. The forming of civil polity, and the giving of expanfion to civil *imperium*, as territorial *dominions* were from time to time extended, was the fpirit of the firft period : war was only the means, or rather the inftrument, of thofe efforts to that end. A direct fpirit of war, a deftroying fpirit, fuch as actuates beafts of prey, was the fpirit of the people, who, at the commencement of the fecond period, over-ran the then cultured and civilized world, and overwhelmed, as with a deluge, all eftablifhments of ancient polity. Any organized idea of government, other than that of the order, difcipline, and conduct, of their armies, entered not into their fyftem. Thefe people had no idea of *civil* government as neceffarily co-extenfive with the

prædopræedominant military *imperium*; no idea of Sovereignty, but as the *external exertion of force of arms*, always held paramount, over the fubordinate command of civil polity : and occafionally exerted, either in aid, or in reftraint and repreffion of it, as the cafe refpecting the fupreme fovereign military power required. * They confidered all civil polity as mere fubordinate arrangement and interior œconomy in a family or tribe, which the community could beft fettle for itfelf ; and under which it would be beft anfwerable to the fovereign power : of what form this polity was, or how adminiftered, was matter of indifference to thefe military fovereigns, fo long as the government, remaining fubordinate, preferved the lands in a ftate capable of anfwering the fupplies demanded of them ; fo long as they preferved the lives and limbs of the individual fubjects as depôts of effective recruits to the army. Under this idea, and with this view only, did the fovereign fuperintend † and make inquifition into

---

* In pace nullus communis eft magiftratus, fed principes regionum atque pagorum inter fuos jus dicunt et controverfias minuunt.

Cæfar de Bell. Gall. lib. 6, 623.

† If the Antiquarian Lawyer inquires into this matter, he will in this fact find the origin of fome of the firft principles of our own law.

B 2   the

the ftate of the government, the property, and the lives of the individuals.

The facts of the hiftory of this univer-fal deluge of Barbarians, as they are ftyled, the operations of this general revolution in the affairs of man, are generally or in-cidentally told by the Greek and Roman writers : but the fources and the firft courfes of thefe people who were the ac-tors in it, lying beyond the *hiftoric horizon*; the *few notices*, which are left refpecting them, being long prior to all chronologic canon ; and the caufes of their abundant population not coming within the fcope of the philofophy of thefe Greek and La-tin writers ; this very important and in-terefting event has been generally viewed with that wonder and aftonifhment, which ftruck the civilized world on the firft ir-ruption of thefe people : and men in ge-neral have rather fat down under this firft impreffion continued, than exerted their faculties in the inveftigation of remote caufes and their operation.

The really philofophic antiquary will not view the irruptions of thefe multitudes of people, as though they dropt from the clouds like a blight of infects, mere fwarms of devourers ; as though they fprang out

of

of the earth—*seges clypiata virorum*. He will not look upon their incursions, as if, like birds of paffage, they flew through the air. He will confider and examine their capacity of moving in a body ; and their œconomy in fupporting that body. He will not be content in ranking thefe people as mere favages ; and in refolving all their operations into mere brutal force. When he inquires, he will find amongft them military training and difcipline, and a *military imperium* formed : he will ob-ferve, in their motions, a regulated fyftem of march and encampment ; a perfectly affured eftablifhment of fupply in provi-fions, forage, and ammunition ; with ade-quate carriage for the whole. He will fee, at the head of thefe, leaders of fpirit and ftrength of mind, equal to the holding their ferocious officers and foldiers in fub-ordination ; and to the maintaining their command: he will find them habile in reafoning experience ; and equal to the conducting of this their command to its point of fervice, in all circumftances, and in every duty of generalfhip ; and finally, he will find them equal to meet in the field the firft and beft generals of the civi-lized world.

He that fees thefe things in this light, will not be content with a fuperficial view :

the

the philofophic antiquary will collect, in the due fpirit of inveftigation, all the facts and fragments of facts, as they lie fcattered amidft the mafs of hiftoric ruins; and as they lie buried, and overgrown by the weeds of fable : He will, as a philofopher, analyfe the principles of the human Being, in its proceffion to civilization ; and in its progreffive, ftationary, or declining, population : He will try thefe principles by facts as they have actually exifted in one place and time ; and compare them by analogy with what is related, although but in part, to have exifted in another ; and, finally, will become able to explain even thofe fragments of facts by thefe principles, fo as to recompofe them, into fome femblance at leaft, of their original exiftence.

The artift who is acquainted with the parts and members of architecture, and knows their fcientific forms and proportions, each under their refpective order, will, if he finds but the fragments of an edifice, be able to pronounce of what order, ftyle, and magnitude, that building was : and if he fhould find all the parts, although in the confufion of broken ruins, he will be able to put them together again, and to re-edify that mafs of antiquity to its original ftructure.

Juft

Juſt ſo may the philoſophic antiquary (* man having his peculiar *order* in the nature of his being, and his decided modes and *modules* in the proceſſion of his exiſtence) recompoſe the hiſtory of the human race by the principles of its ſyſtem : for, although ſome parts may be loſt, others broken, and all lying in confuſion of ruin ; yet, from a combination that has reference to a whole, as it may be found in nature, ſuch a general ſemblance of the original may be reſtored, as ſhall anſwer all the purpoſes of practical and uſeful information.

This treatiſe now, as an eſſay attempting to explain, apply, and give example of, this propoſition, proceeds in the line, and according to the rule, it hath lain down, to inveſtigate, and ſtate who theſe people were ; what they were ; whence they came ; and by what routs, and in what manner (when they advanced to invade the old world) they made their irruptions.

* —— veræ numeroſque moduſque ediſcere vitæ.
Horat. Ep. 2. v. 144. lib. 2.

—————— ————— ————— cur non
Ponderibus moduliſque ſuis ratio utitur ?
Id. Sat. 3. v. 77. lib. 1
Metire ſe quemque ſuo modulo ac pede verum eſt.
Id. Epiſt. 7. 498. lib. 1.

Before

Before we enter upon the examination of thefe points, it will be ufeful, if not neceffary, to fettle the *hiftoric horizon*, (if I may ufe that expreffion,) as thereby the antiquary will be able to diftinguifh hiftory from fable ; and even in fable to find a clue to hiftory.

* The Northern coafts of Europe to the North-eaft of the Elb were not at all known +. The Euxine fea was very little, if at all, navigated in the earlieft times ‡. There was no certainty about the Cafpian, which was fuppofed to be a great bay of the Northern ocean : as was alfo the Euxine §.

The ‖ Scythian clans of the Roxolani, dwelling on the North of the vale of the

* Τὰ δὲ πέραν τῦ Ἄλβιος τὰ πρὸς τῷ Ὠκεανῷ παντάπασιν ἄγνωςα ἡμῖν ἐςίν. Strabo, lib. 7. p. 294.

+ ὅτε γὰρ τῶν προτέρων εὐδίας; ἴσμεν τὸν παράπλεν τῦτον πεποιημένος πρὸς τὰ ἑώϊνὰ μέρη, τὰ μέχρι τῦ ςόματος τῆς Κασπίας Θαλάσσης, ὅθ' οἱ Ῥωμαῖοι προσῆλθόν πω εἰς τὰ περαιτέρω τῦ Ἄλβιος.· ὡς δ' αὔτως ὐδὲ πεζοὶ παρωδεύκασιν ὐδένες. vide porro quod fequitur. Strabo, ibid.

‡ Strabo referring to Eratofthenes (who is faid to quote Damaftes, who, again, cites Bergæus Euemerus) fays— Τὸ παλαιὸν ὅτε τὸν Εὔξεινον θαῤῥεῖν τινὰ πλεῖν. Lib. 1.

§ Ἁπλῶς δὲ οἱ τότε τὸ πέλαγος τὸν Ποντικὸν ὥσπερ ἄλλον τινὰ Ὠκεανὸν ὑπολάμβανον. Strabo, Lib. 1. p.21.

‖ Οἰκῦσι ἐπὶ τῆ Βορεάδος ὕπατοι τῶν γνωρίμων Σκυθῶν, Ῥωξολάνοι, κοτιώτεροι ὄντες τῶν ὑπὲρ τῆς Βρετανικῆς ἐσχάτων γνωριζομένων ἤδη δὲ τὰ ἐπέκεινα διὰ ψύχος ἀοίκητά ἐςι. Strabo, Lib. 2. p. 114.

Bo-

Boryſthenes, were the moſt extreme northern people who were known ; for, the regions beyond them, although in a parallel more to the South than many parts of Britain, which were known to be inhabited, were ſuppoſed to be uninhabitable on account of the extreme cold. Such is the Northern *hiſtoric horizon*, which the ancients * more preciſely fixed at 54°, 27' north lat. This was the extent of the precife geographic knowlege of the ancients †; all beyond this was unknown, and ſuppoſed to be a region of inhoſpitable cold and darkneſs, the *fabulous region*.

The more remote ancients, as ‡ Homer and Heſiod, although they ſeem to have known more than they explain, take up

---

* Strabo, book 2. p. 135, ſays, that the regions beyond the latitude where the longeſt day is of 17 hours were uninhabitable, on account of the extreme cold, and therefore ἐκ ἐπὶ χρήσιμα τῷ Γεωγραφῷ ἐτί.

† Ὑπερβορέων περὶ ἀνθρώπων ἐτέ τι Σκυθοὶ λέγεσιν ὀυδὲν, ἐτὲ τίνες ἄλλοι τῶν ταύτῃ ὀικημένων εἰ μὴ ἄρα Ἰσσήδαες· ὡς ἐγὼ δοκέω ἐυδ' ἐῦτοι λέγεσιν ἐδὲν. Herod. l. 4. c. 39.

‡ Strabo, Lib. 3. p. 149. ſpeaking of Homer as taking up fable where knowledge ends, ſays, κάθαπερ κὴ τὴς Κιμμεριίες εἰδὼς ἐν βορείοις κὴ ζέφυείοις οἰκησαήλας τοποις; τοῖς κατὰ τὸν Βόσπορον Ἰδρυσεν ἀυτές, πρὸς τῷ ἄδῃ.

And Heſiod. Τιτῆνες γαίας πέρην χάεος ζοφεροῖο.
Theog. v. 814
ὑπὸ χθονὸς ἐυρυοδείης· v. 717.

---

the

the vulgate current idea of their cotempo-
raries, and fuppofe all beyond this horizon to be beyond the bounds of the earth ;
nay, beyond chaos ; to be the region of
Hades, and fubterranean : they called this
region, however, *Tartaros* *, by the name
of a people and country which really exifted. This unknown land, defcribed as beyond the extreme bounds of, or beneath,
the earth, was the fabulous habitation of
a people known to the ancients only in
fable. Thefe were the Cymri, Cimmerii
or Cimbri of the early ages †, the fuppofed children of the fon of Japetus or
Japheth, which perfou, although not
named by Hefiod, is perfonally named by
our Holy Scriptures, Gomer : and who by
the allegory of his holding up the heavens
with his head and arms in thefe parts, is
pictured as the origin of this race : as the
founder, and protecting God, having his
head enveloped in clouds and darknefs.
This fragment of hiftory, preferved by
Hefiod, although by him exprefled in
fable, is confirmed by the Book of Genefis
as hiftory.

---

* —————— ἰς Τάρταρον τεράσσα.
　　　　　　　　Hefiod. Theog. v. 721.

† Τῶν πρὸς τ' Ἰαπἔλᾶιο παἴς ἴχετ' οὐρανὸν εὐρὺν
'Εςηκὼς, κεφαλῆτι κ̓ ἀκαμάτῃσι χείρεσσιν.
　　　　　　　　Hefiod. Theog. v. 746.

　　　　　　　　　　　　Τα

To this country the Titans are, after the fuppreffion of their rebellion againft Jove, Jao, or Javah, fuppofed to have been driven, as to a prifon.

The Cymri, or *Tribes,* (which is the real meaning of the appellative,) were fuppofed to be the moft ancient as well as the moft northern people ; yet people originally of fable, being the defcendants of the firft fon of this Japetus, or Japheth.

There were two other nations of the fame race and family, the Teuts (pronounced Teyts), called, by the Hellenifts, * Titans; and the Oïm, Goyem, or Gygim, thefe two nations occupied a fecond and more foutherm graduation of region, not beyond, but on the *extreme bounds* or frontiers of the earth (as will be fhewn) under the government of the God-teus, or Got-teus, or Κότ]υς; and of Gyges. It will appear that thefe two people are defcendants of fuppofed*younger*fons of this Japetus or Japheth, which fons were, in the language of the Eaft, in the language of the Gods, called, the one Tu-baal, and the other Magog. The etymology of Tubaal and Gotteus expreffes one and the fame perfonal character: and Magog is

* Teyt-anes, the children, or progeny, of Teu:, Teyt, Tis, Dis, &c.

the

the radical appellative Gog, Goy, or Oï, with the prefix *Ma* added to it, meaning the hither Gojïm, as diftinctive of their relative fituation refpecting the Afiatic people, by whom they were fo called: exactly as the Ma-daïm with the fame prefix *Ma*: and the Maffagetæ with the prefix *Mais*. One branch of thefe defcendants of Oï, Oj, Goy, Goj, or Gog, (or as the Greeks pronounced the name Gyges,) were the original inhabitants of Troïa, or Troja, an appellative formed from Tré, and Oïm, or Ojim, fignifying the diftrict or region of the Oïm or Ojim. Thefe were by the Hellenic colonifts called *Sons of the Earth*, or men, as diftinguifhed from thofe colonifts from the South, who called themfelves *Children of the Sun*, or Gods, which the word Hellenoi fignifies, meaning no more than, by an eaftern metaphor, the northern and fouthern people.

In hiftoric reafoning it comes to the fame concluding truth, whether a people are confidered by the antiquary as deriving down their progeny by *actual generation* from fome fuppofed firft father of the race, whofe head, like that of Japetus, is above the clouds, that is, whofe origin is unknown: or whether they trace back their hiftorical genealogy to fome imaginary founder and protector of their race;

fome

some god whom they worship : and therefore, in the account which this essay will
attempt to give of the *original inhabitants*
of Europe, it will first trace back(through
such fragments of history as the ruins afford) the race to its supposed first progenitor or founder ; and thence derive down
the history of its generations, and the
processions of its population and inhabitancy, to that period which fixes each
branch as a distinct nation in the great
drama of history. The author of this
essay hopes he does not wantonly adopt
profane ideas in supposing that he can see
this method observed in sacred story.

Having traced up, by the means of profane history, as it stands confirmed by the
sacred, the origin of the Cymri, or Cimmerii, to Gomer the son of Japheth, I
will endeavour to trace, even in utter
darkness beyond the *historic horizon*, their
migrations, and the processions of their
generations to those * Cimbri, who possessed the north-western and most extreme
western bounds of Europe.

The apologue of another race of people, as not yet supposed to have emerged

* Κιμμερίας τὰς Κίμβρας ὀνομασάντων τῶν Ἑλλήνων.
Strabo, lib. 7. p. 293.

from

from the fubterranean *Tartaros*, and to have advanced upon the face of the earth; as not yet having *hiftoric exiftence*, plainly refers, and directly too, when it points them out as coming forth from the regions eaft of the Euxine, to thofe clans or hords of eaftern * oigurs, then unknown, which in after-periods advanced upon the hiftoric world, under the appellatives of Tartars Huns, Alans, &c. &c. &c. This fragment imperfect as it is, and although coming in fo queftionable a form as fabulous, is yet hiftoric. Thefe tribes were then actually beyond the utmoft bounds of the *hiftoric horizon*, beyond the extremities of the known earth, they were under the earth. We will at prefent leave thefe Tartar people in thefe eaftern parts of this parallel of latitude beyond the hiftoric horizon. There let them reft the due period of their fœtation in the womb of time: whilft this effay endeavours to purfue, in the fame parallel weftward, the progreffions and inhabitancy of the Cymri, Cimmerii, or Cimbri of the Weft.

As thefe will be beft defcribed in their courfes conjunctly with the generations of the Teuts and Gojim (the fuppofed defcendants of Cot-teus and Gyges) running in the next parallel; we will, from the

* Vide Van Strahelnbergh.

fame ancient account, and at the fame
time, defcribe this region and people. As
the Cymri were beyond the fuppofed extreme bounds of the earth : * *Where
night and day bordering upon, and within
call of each other, hold their alternate
courfes, each for its determined period.
Where, whilft day is abroad for her period of months upon the face of the earth,
night remains confined within her dark man-
fions : and whilft night, in her turn, and
for her like period, envelopes the earth,
day is totally withdrawn from it, waiting
for her returning feafon:* fo the next
region, fuppofed to be at, or on, the extremities of the earth, is fuppofed to be
the line of inhabitancy of the Teuts and
Gojim. The antiquary will obferve,
that this defcription marks exactly
the regions within the polar circle; but
will find at the fame time, that the
defcription takes too high a latitude for

* ——— ὅϑι Νύξ τε ϗ Ἡμέρα ἄσσον ἰᾶσαι
Ἀλλήλας προσέειπον, ἀμειβόμενοι μέγαν ἀδὸν
Χάλκεον· ἡ μὲν ἔσω καταβήσεται, ἡ δὲ θύραζε
Ἔρχεται, ἀδέ ποτ' ἀμφοτέρας δόμος ἐντὸς ἐέργει·
Ἀλλ' αἰεὶ ἑτέρη γε δόμων ἔκτοσθεν ἐᾶσα
Γαῖαν ἐπιστρέφεται, ἡ δ' αὖ δόμου ἐντὸς ἐᾶσα
Μίμνει τὴν αὐτῆς ὥρην ὁδᾶ, ἔς' ἂν ἵκηται.
Heſiodi Theog. v. 748.

Trans Suionas aliud mare, pigrum ac propè immotum
quo ciugi cludique terrarum orbem, hinc fides, quod ex-
tremus cadentis jom folis fulgor inortus edurat adeo clarus,
ut fidera hebitet. Tacit, de Mor. Germ. § 46.

the

the inhabitancy which it means to defcribe.

In thefe regions, on the extreme bounds
of the earth, the antiquary will find the
defcendants, the fubjects, or the worfhip-
ers, (juft as the fable pleafes to phrafe it,
for, all mean the fame thing,) of Teus and
Gyges: the latter on the eaftern, the firft
on the weftern, bounds of the Euxine Sea
and Mœotic Lake. He will find them
called, in the vulgate and ordinary narrative, by the *general* Grecian appellative,
* *Scythæ* : as well as by various other *particular* appellatives ; but the learned antiquary may at the fame time trace them up
to their national or family name, Gotti,
Teuts, or Dteufch and Gojim, living under
the dominion of † Cotteus and Gyges.

Thefe two great Hetmen, together
with Briareus, are by Hefiod defcribed as
thofe great officers which the Englifh
would call Lords of the Marches, and the

---

* Σκύθας δὲ Ἕλληνες ὀνόμασαν. This is one inftance of the
application of the general Greek appellative to a people
whofe fpecial national appellative was Σκόλοται. Herod. ib. 4.
c. 6. We fhall, in the courfe of this effay, explain what
the word Σκόλοται fignified.

† Ἔνθα Γύγης Κότ7ος τε κ) ὁ Βριαρέως μεγάθυμος;
Ναίωσιν, φύλακε; πιτοὶ Διὸς αἰγιόχοιο.

Hefiod, Theog. v. 734.

Germans,

Germans, Mark-reeves, or Margreeves; commanding on the frontiers at the extreme boundaries of Hertha, (afterwards called by the Greeks Europa), the kingdom of Jao, Jova, or Javah. The regions which formed this kingdom are, by our H. S. History, called *the Ifles of the Gentiles*; and are defcribed, according to the mode obferved in thofe writings, by the names of the families or nations inhabiting them, as the country of the fons of Javan, Elifha, Tarfhifh, Kittim, Dodonim. [Genefis, ch. x. ver. 4.] This dominion, by this defcription, includes Spain, Greece, Theffaly, and Thrace, to the utmoft bounds of Kittim, Κετίας, or Getæ, north ; which is in faĉt the very boundary which we have defcribed. The Antiquary cannot here but obferve how the S. Hiftory coincides with and confirms the *faĉt*, which had been commonly received as fabulous. The portrait given by fable of thofe two great land-officers, and of Briareus, or Ægêon, the marine officer commanding on the Euxine and Mœotic, as having an hundred hands, can mean neither more nor lefs than their being Centreeves or Hetmen, commanding the Centuries or Hundreds of the tribes on thefe boundaries. And thus, in faĉt, doth the fober lan-

C   guage

guage of philofophic hiftory defcribe them,
as may be feen in Palæphatus *.

The nations, who traced up their origin
to or in the language of ancient times,
were the children of Cottys, or the Gott-
teus, Teut, Teyt, Teys, Tis, Dis, (for
all are the fame,) are fuppofed to have
taken from this imagined progenitor their
general family-name, Teuts, Dteufch, or
Dteyfch. Such is the train of genealogic
hiftory : whilft that of fimple etymology
may as naturally fuppofe this name
derived from † Thiot, or Theod, Thyd,
or Thyt, juft as Cimmerii and Cimbri
did from Cymri, both terms, as well as
the term *Ach*, fignifying, in the collective
number, tribes or the community of people, or the race in general. By thefe appellatives the ancient uncivilized tribes of
men defcribed themfelves, until taking
their ftation amongft the civilized communities of the earth they affumed a defcrip-

---

*Φασὶν ἐν περὶ τούτων, ὡς ἴσκον ἐκαλον χεῖρας, ἄνδρες ὄντες· πῶς
δὲ ἐκ εὔηθις το τοιᾶτον ; τὸ δὲ ἀληθὲς ἔπως τῇ πόλει ὄνομα Ἑκατοι-
χειρία, ἐν ᾗ ἔκεν ἦν δὲ πόλις της νῦν καλυμένης Ὀρεστιάδος· ἔλεγον
ἐν οἱ ἄνθρωποι Κότιος κỳ Βριαρέως κỳ Γύγης οἱ Ἑκατοντοχείρες, βοη-
θήσαντες τοῖς Θεοῖς, αὐτοὶ ἐξηλασαντῶς Τιτάνας ἐκ τῦ Ὀλύμπυ.
Παλαιφάτος περὶ ἀπισῶν Ἱστορίαν.

† Thiod populus, univerfitas ; fcribitur alias Thiud,
Thyd, Thiaud.
I. Ihrè Gloffarium Sueo-gothicum.

tive

tive appellation, or national name. When
they were firſt known to the Hellenic coloniſts, theſe appellatives, and this of Thiod
or Teut in particular, was ſuppoſed to be,
according to the univerſal way of reaſon-
ing about names, a *genealogic* name derived from ſome firſt progenitor, Teut,
Teyt, or Tit; theſe Helleniſts, therefore,
in their oriental idiom called them Tit-
anes, the ſons of, or race deriving from
Tit, as a ſtream from its ſource.

In a ſimilar manner from the term *Ach*,
ſignifying, and expreſſive of, the idea of
the collective tribe, race, or people, ſeveral of the tribes inhabiting Greece, Theſ-
ſaly, Thrace, and the regions to the north
of theſe had particular names impoſed on
them by the Hellenic ſettlers, viz. Ach-
αιοι. The tribe Oïm ; Thraci, Tr'-acks ;
Daci, Die-acks ; hence alſo with the prefix *Es* *, ſignifying beyond, or remote, beyond ſome relative line of boundary, was
formed the particular appellative Es-achs
or 'Sachs, or 'Sacæ, the extreme tribes
on the eaſt ; and 'Sachs, or 'Saxones, the
extreme *ſettled* tribes of the Weſt.

---

* 'Eς in the Northern language became ἰκ and ἰξ in the
Greek ; and *Ex*, and in ſome inſtances *Es*, in Latin.

Hiſtory

* Hiftory informs us that thefe Titans (Scythians, as they were alfo afterward called by the Greeks) became more numerous, powerful, and warlike, than the elder and more northern tribes, the Cymri ; and drove them from their original inhabitancy, different ways, fome of them beyond the bounds of the *hiftoric horizon* Weft and North-weft, whilft they themfelves continued the proceffions of their generations and inhabitancy along the next parallel of latitude, that is, along the extreme bounds of the hiftoric horizon. The Scutes, Teuts, and Cotti, are accordingly found progreffive, and advance along the vale of the Boryfthenes ; and on the borders of the Sinus Codanus † from the South eaft to the South-weft. The Cymri in the continuation of their generations and habitancy between the Mœotic Lake (where they firft merged into darknefs, and were loft to hiftory, being beyond its horizon, in the allegoric language, driven *off the face of the earth)* and the Cimbric Cherfonefus and ifles of the Baltic, where they emerged again into the hiftoric horizon, muft have dwelt in or paffed through

* Herodotus.
† Regnum Cimmeriorum, vel Cimbrium, vel Guttiam, vel Jut in appellamus. Ita duplex eft Auftralis et Borealis : p a Saxonibus ad urbes Ripenfam et Codilgenfam ex-
LYSCANDER.

the

the fteps of Tartary, and the Ruffias, defcending down the waters of the Dwina and other rivers, running hence into the Baltic. This courfe was afterward known to the Hunns in ages prior to thofe when they got upon the Danube and attacked the Romans. This courfe, by different routes, was well known in the early ages of the ancient world, to the *trading adventurers* of the great commercial people of thofe days. Thefe bold adventurers pufhed their enterprizes weftward to the Atlantic ocean. They, as all fimilar adventurers do at this day, concealed the particulars of their routes. Therefore, although the Hiftorians and Geographers had a general information that there were fuch *courfes*; yet thefe being concealed beyond the hiftoric horizon, they were totally ignorant of the particular routes. They had picked up fome general information of the number of days journey, which thefe traders advanced up thefe rivers; and they made the geographical meafurement of the length of thefe rivers by fuch. This courfe up the Tanais, over the height of the land, down the rivers which run into the Baltic, and hence to the Atlantic ocean, is the courfe which the * fabled navigators

of

* In the Treatife on the Study of Antiquities, which was
C 3 publifhed

of the Argos are suppofed, in the Argonautics of Orpheus, to have taken.

Whilft thefe Cymri remained between thefe two points, and beyond the hiftoric horizon, all knowledge of them was fabulous, and they were called Hyperboreans. They came forward again to hiftory in the isles of the Baltic, in the Cimbric Cherfonefus, then an ifland, and in the Weftern ifles of the ocean, under their general appellative Cymri, pronounced with the digamma Cim-v-ri or Cim-b-ri.

publifhed in 1782, I ventured to fuggeft that the Argonautic expedition was, at the bottom, a map of the commerce of the ancients, formed into a fable, and wrought into an heroic poem. And now, in 1793, upon a revifion of this fable, as written in the Argonautics of Orpheus and of Apollonius Rhodius, I feel myfelf confirmed in that conjecture.

The feveral perfons concerned in this drama were of fo many different countries and ages, that they could hardly in fact be brought together as fhip-mates in the fame voyage, except in fable. Befides, the fable has reference to two very different voyages, in very different courfes; there is alfo reafonable ground [vide Gefner de navigationibus Phœnicum, Lact. I, § 3. alfo Bochart and Burman's Catalogue of the Argonauts] to fuppofe that Ancæus, the fabled pilot of the Argos, was fome famous Phœnician navigator. The two different courfes mentioned in the Argonautics of Orpheus, and in thofe of Apollonius Rhodius, were, however, both ufed courfes of the commerce of the ancients. The trade up the Danube was for Chittim-wood, and for flaves, from the Getæ and Davi, and I believe alfo for grain. The trade up the Boryfthenes and Tanais, &c. &c. was for peltry, furs, and amber.

I

The

The firft account which the Antiquary will meet with concerning thefe people the Cymri or Cimbri, and the Teuts or Teytifch, as afterwards of the Hunns, either in their clans, or as a nation, either as roving predatory parties on land, or as naval pirates on the feas, is recorded in the Gothlandic annals, compofed from, and founded on, authentic Runic monuments, and on tradition, which it was part of their civil inftitution to preferve and tranfmit by the Vyfur or the Scaldri. The authority and teftimony of thefe moft early hiftories (although deformed with poetic fables) is of equal at leaft, I own I think of fuperior, credit, to the hiftory of the firft periods of Greek and Roman hiftory, equally deformed with fables.

Both thefe people are defcribed as become Sea-rovers, or Vics, (Vickanders, Wickingers, Fieds, and Pieds,) tranflated, by thofe who knew the meaning of the word, into Piratæ ; but miftaken by thofe who did not know its meaning, for the Latin word Pieti *.

By

* Nothing can be more eftranged from, or ignorant of, the fact, when the Picts are fuppofed to be fo called from their *painting* their bodies. The Britons certainly did, fo did originally many, if not moft of the Thracians and Illy-

rians,

By the neceffity which thefe tribes found of drawing their fubfiftence from the ocean, and from the nature of their fituation, they became fifhermen and navigators: from thefe circumftances they became alfo populous : from the conftant training and neceffity of command, to concenter and give unity of action to men following their occupation in bodies, they naturally organized into frames of government ; and, from the courfe of their predatory excurfions, fell into fubordination to military commands. They thus in time became, under their *Wiggans* and *Thagens*, naval warlike powers. They not only made incurfions reciprocally into each others borders, but, in train of time and events, into Scotland, England, Belgia, and the fhores of Aquitaine. They paffed up the Rhine, and other rivers of Germany and Gaul. They fent out and eftablifhed colonies in thefe regions, efpecially in Scotland, under their *Vics* or *Wiggans* ; and in Ireland, and Aquitaine, and Spain, under their *Thagens*, and as Vettones in Spain : finally, after various predatory irruptions even in-

rians †, κατάγιdιοι [tattoo'd] δ' ὁμοίως τοῖς ἄλλοις Ἰλλυρίοις κ̀ Θρᾷξι. But there is no account, or the moft diftant hint, that the Pics or Picts did fo.

† Strabo, Edit. Cafaub. 1585. Lib. 7. p. 318.

to Italy, they advanced in power even to the attempting the conqueſt of Rome it-ſelf; and actually in the end, under their names Cimbri, Teutones, Goths, Wandals, &c. overturned and totally annihilated the Weſtern Roman Empire. The courſes of the particulars of which proceſſion of power and action will be ſeen in the ſequel.

As the Antiquary, in the courſe of his enquiries into theſe ſubjects, will meet repeatedly with ſome general terminations, which are annexed to the names of the bodies or ſwarms, migrating from theſe clans of people, both thoſe of the Teytiſch as well as thoſe of the Cymric tribes, ſuch as *ingi*, *aitæ*, or *atæ*, and *ones*, or with the digamma *vones*. It comes in here in the regular courſe of philoſophic analyſis, and will hereafter ſpare much repeated trouble to the reader, to explain the nature and meaning of theſe terminations.

The word *ing* and *ingi* when affixed as a termination to any patronymic, ſignifies ſon or ſons, deſcendants, or *of the race*. This termination is rather more peculiar to the Teytiſch family.

Aitæ,

Aitæ, Haid, or Hait, is a Cymric termination, and fignifies, in its firſt fenſe, a fwarm of bees, from *heddio* to fwarm ; in its applied fenſe, fignifies an emigrating body of ſuch or ſuch a race or clan, as it becomes the termination to the name of. The word Ætt in the Sueco-gothic language, Aita in the Camb : Haite and Hayte in Fris: Attya in the Hung : Aiti in the Finl: and Aitea in the Lapland, are all fynonymous.

Ones, from Wonen, derived from Woɡan to dwell ; and ὡνες the Greek termination from ῞Ωον teᴄtum, (ſignifying the fame thing,) denotes, when added as a termination to any name of a people, or rather colony of a people, that ſuch were become fettled *dwellers*. This termination is moſt in uſe with the Teytiſch Family.

By annexing the termination *ingi*, to the word Pıɡa, or Wiga (pronounced, and written alſo, variouſly, Wig, Vic, Fiᴄt, Piᴄt, Peaght, Veᴄt, and Wight or Vet, a Warrior, or War-captain, and in eminence *viᴄtor)*, come, Wickings, Wittingi, the band of warriors or conquerors : by annexing the termination *ones* to the fame appellative, the fame people are called Viᴄtones, Piᴄtones, Vettones;

tones; by annexing *ingi* to the Teuts, or Teutfchs, come the Teutingi, Teuthingi, and fignifies emigrants from, or defcendants of, the Teuts or Teytfch : by annexing *ones* to the fame name, the words Teutones and Teuthones are made, and means the fame people become fettled *dwellers.* In like manner 'Sacæ, 'Sachs, and 'Saxones; Gutts, Jutts, and Goths, make Guttingi, Juttingi, Guthingi, and Gothingi. The Greeks had the fame termination fignifying the fame thing. The Haliz*ones* are the people who dwelt beyond or on the other bank of or beyond the river Halys ['Αλιζώνας ἐκἰὸς τῦ "Αλυος. Strabo, lib. 12, p. 552.] The Antiquary will find many inftances of the application of this termination *ones* amongft the Teutfch nations, fometimes with the digamma w and v, as Inge *v*ones, the inhabitants of the Ings or Low Countries; but moftly without the digamma, as Ifte-ones, and Hermi-ones, &c. and the Treres, and * Trere-ones. By adding the termination aite, or ates, to the word Fen or Ven, is made the appellative of the Venaitæ, a people who fettled in the fwampy fens and marfhy coafts. By compounding aitæ with the word *Cyn* prefixt (which fignifies fo prefixt, primary or firft) is made the appellative Cynaid,

___

* Strabo, lib. i.

or Cynhait, the firſt or ſpring ſwarm, or
princely ſwarm, which became the appellative of a colony ſettled on the extreme
weſtern coaſts of Europe, mentioned by
Herodotus, and by him named *Κυνήται or
Cyn-aitæ. By annexing this term *ait* or
haïd to the name Vict, Pict, or Fict, is
made the word Fictaid, the appellative by
which the Welch called the ſettlements
and ſettlers of the Picts : by compounding
this word, ſignifying ſwarm, or tribe,
with the prefix Ma—, is made the appellative of the hither-tribes, clans, or ſettlers mentioned by Camden, under the
appellative Maaittæ, diſcriminating thoſe
tribes who lived on the ſouth ſide the
Highlands of Calidonia. The people, who
afterwards aſſumed the national name
Lydi, were alſo originally called by the relative appellation Maiônes or the hither
inhabitants. Αυδοὶ ὀι ποτε Μηῶνες, Strabo,
Lib. 11. p. 185. Hence alſo the Tanai-
tæ or Tagenaid) near the Mœotic. Hence
the 'Sarmatæ? hence the Attrab-ates,
the Cal-ates, and Callones ; hence alſo in
Aquitania the Nann-ates, the Cocoſ-ates,
Voc-ates, Tarun-ates, Toloſ-ates, the
Eluſ-ates, Sibutz-ates, et Soli-ates. The

---

* Ἀρξάμενος ἐκ τῶν Κελτῶν ὁι ἐσχατοι πρὸς Ἡλία δυσμέων,
μετὰ Κυνήτας, ὀιχυσι τῶν ἐν τῇ Εὐρώπῃ.
        Herod. Lib. 4. c. 49.

Anti-

Antiquary will alfo find it ufeful, in his etymology, to remember the prefixes Ma—, Mais—, Mafs— ; and Es; the three former always, when prefixed to the name of a people or region, means the pofition on the hithermoft fide of fome relative mark or line ; and the latter Es, a pofition over, beyond, or on, the farther fide of fuch relative. The Greeks ufed both thefe, and efpecially ες, as in έσχατος and έσπερος, &c.

When now this effay proceeds in its attempt, as in a prefatory commentary, to collect the fcattered fragments of the firft progreffive fettlements of the Cymri, Cimmerii, or Cimbri ; and whilft it only endeavours to trace this one branch of the firft inhabitants of Europe, through the proceffions of their generations and habitancy ; I muft hope it may not be underftood as though I aim in this effay to write their hiftory. The purpofe of this refearch is not to form an hiftory, but to trace fuch conjectural lines, and to lay before the Antiquarian reader fuch theorems ftated thereupon, as may give, in fome degree, lead to his learned inveftigations, and afford fome means of recompofing the broken and fcattered fragments

to

to fome femblance of their original actual
ftructure.

Thefe Cymric as well as the Teytifch
tribes, or clans, were, originally, when
known in the Eaft, on the coafts and
borders of the Euxine Sea, and Mœotic
Lake *, rovers and predatory free-booters.

Thofe who dwelt to the Northward †
on the waters, in the marfhes, and fens,
were ‡ fifhermen § and 'Ιχθυόφαγοι, di-

---

* Ποσειδώνιος, κ̣ ὁ κακῶς, εἰκάζει ὅτι λήςρικοι ὄντες κ̣ πλάνητες οἱ
Κιμϐροι, κ̣ μέχρι τῶν περὶ τὴν Μαιῶτιν ποιήσαιͻ ςρατείαν.
Strabo, lib. vii. p. 293.

† κατήκοντες ἐπὶ θαλάσσην. Herod. lib. iv. c. 13.

‡ Οἱ δ' ἐν τοῖς ἕλεσιν ἰχθυοφαγᾶσιν· ἀμπέχονται δὲ τὰ τῶν
φωκῶν δέρματα τῶν ἐκ θαλάτης ἀνατρεχᾶσῶν· Οἱ δὲ πεδινοὶ καί
περ ἔχοντες χώραν, ὂ γεωργᾶσιν, ἀλλ' ἀπὸ προϐάτων κ̣ ἰχθύων
ζῶσι Νομαδικῶς, κ̣ Σκυθικῶς. Ἐςὶ γάρ τις κ̣ κοινὴ ἡ δίαιτα πάν-
των τῶν τοιαύτων. Strabo, lib. xi. p. 513.

Detracta velamina [fciz ferarum] fpargunt maculis:
pellibufque belluarum quas *exterior* oceanus atque ignotum
mare gignit. Tacit. de Mor. Geom, § 17.

Εἴμι δ' ἐγὼ γεγαυῖα μέσον θνήτα τε θεᾶστι
Νύωϑης ἐθαάτης, πατρός δ' ἀν Κηταφάγοιο.

Fragm. byzn in Hierophylæ, apud Paufaniam, lib. x.

§ ' ... θύ ... ἅλες δὲ ἐπὶ τῷ ςόματι οὗτ' αὐτό-
μ ... τ' ... μεγάλα ἀνάκανθα. τὰ ἀνταλαᾶς
κ ... Τοςάχιυσιν. Herod Lib iv. c. 53.

There was alfo a fifhery of a leffer fort of fifh called
Πέλαμις, which was a fifh of paffage, coming from the North
in great fhoals, which the inhabitants of the Euxine caught
for falting. See Strabo, lib. vii. p. 340. There was
alfo a confiderable fifh in Epirus. Ibid. p. 327.
Great ... which the Greeks traded to
... αἱ ταρίχειαι. Ibid, p. 311.

ftinguifhed

ftinguifhed by their occupation and food from the hunter and paftor. The places which thefe Northern people occupied abounded with fifh: and they had learnt the art of curing and preferving it by falt *; which provifion, fo prepared, they called by a technical name *Taracheufis*. Situation and circumftances point out to man the occupation which is to fupport his life. Man is, in the natural courfe of his being, always the fame thing, under the fame circumftances. The Cimbri driven from their original fituation into the fame kind of fituation in the iflands of the Sinus Codanus, in the † Cimbric Cher-

---

* See the laft note in the preceding page.

† This was originally, and continued to be in the earlieft times, an ifland feparated from the main-land or continent. The people, who came from thefe parts to Calidonia and Iteland, were, by the Caledonians and Irifh, faid to come from *Lock-Lyn*, the ifland in the lake. See on this point the very learned Memoire of the Abbe Mann, wherein he, from fact, defcribes the ancient ftate of the Low Countries, as alfo his *Carte-hydrographique* in the firft volume of the Memoirs of the Imperial and Royal Academy at Bruxelles. He takes from the fact a fcientific analyfis of the levels and nature of the tides on that coaft. He alfo makes a collective inveftigation of difcoveries of the veftiges of ports and havens in parts, far within what is now land : hence, he not only proves that the tides muft have overflown thefe levels, and that this tract muft have been fea ; but he actually traces the line of the fhore, properly called the Saxon fhores, as it ran at that time. This very learned, fcientific, and ingenious, treatife, fhould be read by every Antiquary and Hiftorian, who wifhes to underftand the topography and geography of the Roman Hiftory.

fonefus,

fonefus, and in the Weftern ifles, became, of courfe, a marine and naval people. If at the fame time the Antiquary examines the fituation of the Teutfch tribes on the fea coafts of the main land, ; ftill upon their flanks on the South), he will find them in a fituation fomewhat fimilar, though not the fame: He will find them under circumftances which would naturally, and did in fact, make them *watermen* and fifhermen; but not fuch as to lead directly to marine navigation. The Cimbri dwelt in the fea: the Teuts, or Teyts, in rivers, on lakes, in vliets, fens, and marfhes. The Cimbri, therefore would, as they did, firft become *a naval power.* And, although hitherto they had been repreffed by the Teuts, they did, in this character, and by this power, recoil upon their oppreffors; and, in procefs of events, acquired the afcendant power of conqueft over them.

As we have faid that it is the fite and circumftances of a country which originally form the occupation, and, in confequence, the character, of the inhabitants; the antiquary, perhaps, may not be unwilling to review the accounts, which may be collected, of the antient ftate of the country, forming the North-weftern fhores,

fhores, called afterwards the Saxon fhores. For my own part, I do it with the more pleafure, as it confirms the *local* defcription drawn out by my friend the Abbé Mann.

The whole North-weftern part of the continent of Europe, north of the line of high-land, as drawn by that learned Academician from the heights of Bologn, by Bruxelles, Lovain, and Tongres, between Bonne and Cologne, and by Berlin to Dantzig *, was a compound of fens and marfhes; of vliets, lakes, and marine baies, running amidft a country †, in few

* Ambæ nationes (fciz. Fresiorum) Rheono prætexuntur et ambiunt immenfos infuper lacus.
Tacit. de Mor. Ger. § 34.
Eundem Germaniæ finum proximi oceano Cimbri tenent.
Ibid. § 38.
'Saxones gentem in Oceani littoribus, et paludibus inviis fitam.—Paulus Diaon, Lib. xii. § 2.
Sueïonum civitates ipfo in Oceano, præter viros armaque, claffibus valent.—Tacit ut fupra, § 43. Tacitus fays in general of the coaft——Cætera Oceanus ambit latos finus, et infularum immenfa fpatia compleftans, § 1.

† Dives agri provincia [fci. Frefia confinis Juliæ] et pecoribus opulens; ceterum confinis oceano patet humilis, ita ejus folum interdum œftibus eluatur. Qui ne irrumpant, vallo littus omne percingitur: quod fi forte perfregerint, inundant campos, vicos et fita demergunt. Hyeme continuo celatur æftu, ftagni fpeciem prebentibus campis. Unde et in quâ rerum parte locanda fuerit penè ambiguum natura fecit: cùm aliâ anni parte navigationis patiens,

D   alia

few parts, whole year land, except by the defence of banks, or in the iflands. Thofe parts, which were not fo artificially defended, and made land, were covered with water the greateft part of the year, and always at the periods of fpring-tides ; and, even where they were embanked in, they were liable to breaches in their defences *

by

aliâ aratri capax exiftit. Quem paluftrem primùm et humidum longo duravere cultu.

Saxo Grammaticus, lib. iv. He gives the fame account of Frefia Magna. Æftûs refluxionis vis, plus utilitatis an periculi incolis afferat ambiguum eft : fiquidem tempeftatis magnitudine prærupeis æftuariis, quibus apud eos maritimi fluctus intercipi folent, tanta arvis undarum moles, incedere confuevit, ut interdum non folum arvorum culta, verum etiam homines cum penatibus obruat.

Idem in præfat. ad Hiftoriam.

* If a hard gale of wind, at Weft, has blown for fome time before the coming on of the fpring-tides, efpecially thofe of the equinoxes and folftices ; and if that gale changes by the Eaft, as is commonly the cafe at the clearing up of fuch, juft at the time of high water coming in to the German ocean ; from the coincidence of thefe circumftances, the height of the tide, which comes in, rifes from eight to eleven feet above the average level of the low lands, on all fides of this fea; overtops their banks ; and generally breaks them. Perfons converfant with philofophic inquiries will fee [vide Governor Pownall's Treatife on the currents in the Atlantic, printed for Sayer] that fuch a coincidence of circumftances cannot regularly or frequently happen. There are, however, records, in every country on thefe feas, of fuch tides happening repeatedly at times, and thofe not diftant ones. I here refer to the Dykereeve records on both fides this ocean. There was a very ancient tradition that one of thefe great raging tides drowned all the Cimbric

and

by thofe extraordinary raging tides, which
were, and are in our days, repeatedly experienced from time to time, in the Northern ocean ; and which, exceeding and
over-topping all ordinary defence, always
occafion general inundations.

'From the marfhy and fenny nature of
this habitancy the inhabitants had various
appellatives given to them, or affumed
by them ; as Æftui, Ingli, Morini, Vene-

and Teutonic coafts; and gave occafion to that great emigration, the emigrants of which invaded the Roman empire. Strabo mentions it, but not having a local krow-
ledge of thefe feas, and of thefe extraordinary raging tides,
but reafoning from the ordinary flux of the tides, which, he
fays, being a matter of common notoriety, the people muft
have been prepared for, and provided againft, denies the
probability of the fact of fuch an accident. Had he
known, from written and perfonal experience, from which
the writer of this note reafons, the circumftances and effects
of thefe extraordinary tides, whatever credit he might have
given to, or withheld from, this tradition, on other grounds,
he wou'd have been convinced that his reafoning on it was
unfounded.
    It was one of thefe great extraordinary tides in the month
of September, which had well nigh deftroyed the whole of
Julius Cæfar's fleet drawn up on the fhore of Britain.
Thofe naval people who tranfported the army over, being
perfectly acquainted with the nature and fet of the tides,
both ordinary and fpring tides, as appears in the circumftances of the landing, would of courfe, when they drew
their veffels on-fhore, draw them above the flow of the higheft fpring-tides which rife at this feafon ; but thefe extraordinary raging tides, occafioned by the caufes above referred to, exceed and baffle all calculation, as happened
in the accident which befel thefe tranfports.

dæ,

dæ, as alfo Marfi, (Strabo,) or Marfhmen.
We find alfo (according to Lyfcandèr)
Teutomarfi, Storemarfi, Villimarfi, Crem-
pe-marfi, on the Southern borders of Cimbria. When afterwards fome of the Cimbri, in confequence of their irruptions
above referred to, fettled on thefe marine
coafts, they were called Se-cambri (*proximi oceano Cimbri*), in contradiftinction
to the Cimbri Mediterranei.

The geographers and hiftorians gave to
fome of thofe people, who occupied thefe
low land regions, the appellative * *Ingevones*; which word formed of *Ing*, a mea-
dow, and *ónes*, from woner, to dwell,
means the dwellers on the Ings.

Laftly, this country was called Flan-
ders, or rather Vlanders, from Vloan, and
Vliet, overflown meadows : and the people Flan-mannes, or Floan-andres.

+ There would be no end of quoting
authorities for faying that thefe countries
abounded

* Ingevones, quarum pars Cimbri, Teutones, et Chau-
corum Gentes. Plinii. Nat. Hift. Lib. iv. c. 14.
+ Ita pifcibus frequens exiftit, ut haud minus alimentorum
indigenis ; quam agetur omnis exfolvere videatur.—Tantâ
finus

abounded with fiſh, on which, as the great main article of food, the people ſubſiſted ; but it is worth notice *, that they under-ſtood and practiſed the method of boiling ſalt for uſe.

The hiſtory of theſe people is at the ſame time but one continued proof in ex-ample on fact of their abundant popula-tion ; a phyſical conſequence of their cir-cumſtances of life, and of this food.

Tribes of people not yet in a perfect ſtate of civil organization and ſubordina-tion to government, living in ſuch ſitu-ations, and under ſuch circumſtances, be-coming marine hunters and navigators, have always become, in the progreſs of that character, ſea-rovers, and pirates ; in like manner as uncivilized tribes, dwelling in foreſts, and of courſe becoming ſylvan hunters, become prædatory free-booters. They became ſuch, not againſt but on

ſinus omnis piſcium frequentiâ repleri conſuevit, ut inter-dum impacta navigia vix remigii conamen eripiat.
                              Saxo Gramm. Præfat. ad Hiſt.

* This circumſtance is incidentally mentioned by Saxo, giving an account of Hiarno's diſguiſed ſituation, when he prepared to have aſſaſſinated Freidleve. Se quidem deco-quendi ſalis opificem profeſſus inter ſordidioris miniſterii ſamulos ignobilia exequabatur officia. Lib. vi. p. 99.

principle,

principle *, fuch as it was. The fame
fpirit arifing from an internal fenfe of
power (every where the fame) throughout
all natures, which renders the beafts of
prey in the fea, the air, and in the forefts,
deftroyers and devourers of the helplefs,
harmlefs herds, flocks, and fholes, prompted
man (alfo a beaft of prey) to confider thofe
of his own fpecies, who were quiet in
fpirit, and weak in force, as his natural
prey : the fruits of whofe labour, as they
would that of the horfe or ox, they
affumed, from power, a right to take ; and
whofe lives alfo, if fuch croffed upon their
line of adventure, fo as in the leaft to be
obftructive to it, they equally, as a thing
of courfe, took away †. Thefe men bearing upon each other, wherever they met,
in the infufferent fpirit of rivalry, and de-
ciding all competitions and contentions
by blood, lived in a ftate of perpetual war.
Such, in fact, is the equality and the rights
of man. The reafoning ‡, however, of
the

* Quarum ea ratio eft ut inter belluas in agris et faltibus,
in aquis inter pifces, et in æthere inter volatilia, imbecilli-
ora quæque præda funt ferocioribus. Ita ducendum inter
homines barbaros. Crantz. Lib. i. Valdal. c. 7.

† See the ftory of Horwandillus and Collerus, as a ftri-
king example of this. Saxo Gramm. Lib. iii. p. 48.

‡ Sed hæc piraticæ fpecies certis conftat legibus, non
enim quofvis imbelles, aut navigatione victum quærentes,
obruebant,

the beaft-man, the hunter, diftinguifhing
as in his hunt *vermin* from *game*, (a diftinction fubfifting at this day amongft
fportfmen,) fo, in his warfare, the fubjected
labourer from the object of war, led thefe
pirates to diftinguifh, as the proper ob-
jects of their attack, thofe who bore arms
at fea from thofe who only fought and
worked their livelihood therein. It was
a law of arms with them * not to fpoil the
landworker or merchant ; the taking, however, from them, in a cafe of neceffity,
fuch articles of fubfiftence as they wanted,
was an exception : not to rob women,
however opulent; nor to force them
againft their will on-board their fhips ; nor

---

obruebant, ii qui *Vikingorum* titulo fuperbiabant, fed
hoftes faltem, aut eos quos fciebant hâc arte celebres et
præftantes, quique opem ingentem vim bello maritimo con-
quifiverant. Olaus Wormius. Monam. Dan. ad Saxum
Triledenfem, p. 269.

* Colonos vei mercatores nemo fpoliato. quantum verò,
neceffitate urgente, ad alimenta requiritur fumito. Fœmi-
nis quantumvis opulentis nihil eripito ; nec invitas ad naves
educito. Fœminæ et imbecillis ætas captivitate exemptæ.
Herman Torfæi Hift. Nervey, lib. iv. c. 4.

Thefe are fome of the articles of war, or laws of nations (if they may be fo called) amongft a people, for whom
at the fame time, the following regulations alfo were neceffary : Crudis carnibus nemo vefcitor, vel pretextu ex-
preffi per pannum fanguinis lupis quam hominibus fimilio-
rum more. In the fame author I find another regulation
about their arms. Nemini fas gladium ulno longiorem
gerere: cominùs cum hofte congredi oportuit. Id. Ibid.
lib. iv. and vi. c. 3.

to

to reduce the female or the infant to captivity. They thus made a diftinction between piracy and robbery. War, open war againft the one was honourable ; any attack upon the latter, other than ufing, where they wanted fuch, the fruits of their labour, was bafe, and beneath the fpirit of a Vickander ; whofe fword would be difhonoured by the blood of thefe. And from fuch reafoning arofe *their law* of arms and nations.

I need not amafs a heap of quotations to prove that this fpirit and character uniformly exifted in, and actuated fuch people, under fuch circumftances *, who held agriculture a fervile or a feminine labor, and who held it more fuited to the fpirit of a man, to make his acquifitions by his blood rather than by his fweat.

·* ἀργὸν εἶναι κάλλιϛον, Γῆς δὲ ἐργάτην ἀϛιμότατον· τὸ δὲ ζῆν ἀπὸ πολέμε κỳ ληϛύος κάλλιϛον. Herod, lib. v. c. vi.

Τὰς ἀρχιοτάτας πλιν κỳ κατὰ λήϛ καν η εμπορίαν..
Strabo, lib. i. p. 48.
Nec arare terram, aut expectare annum, quam vocare hoftes, et vulnera mereri. Pigrum quinimò et iners videtur, fudore acquirere, quod pofcis fanguine parare.
Tacit. de Mor. Germ.
Antiquitus piratica honefta et licita erat atque in câ fe crebrò reges ipfi, aut eorum liberi exercebant afcitis famofioribus et fortiflimis Athetis. Moris enim olim fuifle refert, regiis filiis regium tribuere ut primum pirati eam exercere cœperunt.
Olaus Wormius de Saxo Tireledenfi.

This

*·This species of sea-rover or pirate, in
the national estimate of character, was held
honourable, and of the first rank. Not
only adventurers of private rank took to
this course for their maintenance, and to
make acquisitions of fortune : but people
of the first rank in the nation, and even
kings themselves engaged in these enterprizes and excursions. Kings used to send
out their best warriours, and oftentimes
their sons on these piratical enterprizes.
And frequently these heirs of kingdoms,
during the lives of their fathers, would
voluntarily desire to be sent out as pirates.
This *imperium Pelagi* was considered, in
those dominions where the crown was par-
tible, as one portion of the inheritance ;
and even some time (there are instances of
this) taken by the eldest son as the first.
There was not an object of more glorious
ambition, for a young hero, than to esta-
blish such a character of enterprize and bra-
very in this line as the most renowned
Vickanders would enlist under, and be-

---

* Antiquitus piratica honesta ac licita erat, atque in eâ
se crebrò reges ipsi aut eorum liberi, exercebantur, ascitis
famolioribus et fortissimis Athletis. Moris enim olim fu-
isse refert. Regiis filiis regium munus tribuere, ut primùm
piraticam exercere cœperunt.
      Olaus Wormius de Saxo Terstedensi.

come

come fellow-warriors to, in his band. This naval command took its rank on a level with the higheſt ſtations of dominion on the land, it was, not only the ſtep to honour, but became the baſis of the pre-dominant power : and therefore was it, that ſome eldeſt ſons of kings, who felt on experience the operation of this power, held this naval command as their own domi-nion, giving to their brothers (as reguli) the dominion of the land. On the other hand, individual adventurers of the loweſt rank having been ſucceſsful, and become powerful in this line, held up themſelves, and were holden up, ſo high in rank of ho-nour, that even kings did not think the giving of their daughters in marriage to them was any diſparagement of rank. Examples of every inſtance here men-tioned are repeatedly found in the hiſtory of theſe people.

Theſe Vics, Vickanders (tranſlated Pi-ratæ), were at firſt, in the earlieſt times, independent bands of adventurers, engaged in cruizing excurſions. According to the example which we find in the courſe of human nature in this ſtate of its progreſ-ſion, to be invariable, ſuch bands formed
them-

themselves under the absolute command of some *one*, under whom they enrolled themselves, and whom they chose as their war-captain, their *Vic.* The Sylvan Indians of America, who know not nor acknowledge any coercive power of civil government, do the same at this day. Their expeditions were only prædatory *, they fixed not any settled establishments, but merely at first took post on such temporary stations as suited the nature and season of their cruize. It appears from such accounts as are collected from runic monuments, in the history of these people, that the Vic and their Vicanders, of the Cymric tribes, were the first, prior to the Teutisch tribes, who made their expeditions on the open seas. Similar bands of the Teutisch tribes did the same afterwards.

* Vide Hist. Hialmari, published by Peringskiold, with a Commentary. Nimirum paludosa initio cum suis incolebat loca, antequam sedes fixas sibi eligere ; cæterum crebrò in piraticas expeditiones profectus, nominis sui gloriam in tantum auxit, ut omnibus quibus rerum gestarum memoriæ describebantur, laudari meruit.

———————Helgo, diviso cum fratre regno,
Maris possessionem sortitus, varios Pelagi recessus
Vago navigationis genere perlustrabat.
                    Saxo Gramm. lib. ii. p. 28.

The

The Cymric Vics began firft to make their incurfions on the Teutifch fettlements amongft the marfhes, fens, and vliets, and on the coafts of thofe tribes who had the name of 'Saxones; and on the eaftern fhores of the Baltic. They then in pro- cefs of time advanced into the ocean, and extended their courfes to the Orcades and Northern coaft of Scotland; thence to the Weftern ifles, and on the Weftern coafts. They were at firft interrupted in their in- curfions upon the coafts of Ireland. The firft fettlement of the Picts, which is the fame appellative as Vic, differently pro- nounced, that was made on the Weftern coafts of Scotland, had been firft attempted on the coafts of Ireland. In later times they farther extended their expeditions to the South-eaftern coafts of Britain, croffing from the Saxon fhores, at the Streights of Dover, to the ifle of Thanet, and to the coafts of the ifle of Wight, or *Vectis*, fo named from their appellative. They alfo extended their cruifes; and in later times (the Teutifch as well as Cimbric fea- rovers) made many fettlements as naval ftations, and afterwards as dwellings, on the Weftern coafts of what is now called France, alfo on the coaft of Spain.

I

The

* The ſhips in which they made theſe excurſions were navigated both by ſails and oars : the leaſt, which one reads of, · carried twelve rowers, and as many fighting men : others an hundred, and ſome one hundred and fifty. They generally made their expeditions with a number of theſe, as a fleet.

One objeƈtion oppoſing itſelf to theſe long voyages ariſes from the idea of the viƈtualling ; but this we have obviated. Another objeƈtion againſt thoſe voyages acroſs the open ſea, beyond the ſight of land from Scandinavia and the Baltic, a paſſage of at leaſt ſeven days in their time, ariſes from the difficulty of conceiving how it was poſſible for theſe navigators to ſet and keep their courſe : an anſwer to that objeƈtion derives from the faƈt, that they did this *by the flight of birds*. It is almoſt unneceſſary to ſtate that birds of paſſage croſs the German ocean twice annually, from the Continent to and from the Britiſh iſles. Founded on this obſervation theſe navigators framed their courſe, in taking their departure, from the courſe

* Hujus minima ratis quæ biſenos veheret nauticor, totidemque remigiis agi poſſit. Saxo Gram. lib. iv. p. 64.
    Canutus Chentelum ſuum ſex millium numerum explentem ſexaginta navigiis cultius apparatis, quolibet centenos armatos capiente, diſtinxit. Saxo. Lib. x. p. 197.

which

which they had obferved thefe birds to take at their emigration. They took with them on-board feveral birds, fometimes hawks, but generally ravens. When having made fome progrefs in this courfe, and out of fight of land, if they were in any doubt of, or wifhed to fet their courfe to the point where the land lay, they let fly one of thefe birds ; thefe, after mounting high aloft in the air, always took their courfe to land, and fo became their pilots; following whofe line of flight the navigators fteered their courfe. The following narrative fupports this. Flocco, an Orcadian, fetting out on a voyage to difcover Iceland, took with him three ravens. In taking his departure from the Orcades, he fet his courfe North ; after being out at fea, he let fly one of his ravens; this returned back to the Orcades : he ftill perfevered in his courfe, and let fly a fecond ; this returned to the veffel : ftill perfifting, he let fly the third ; this went off directly North, and never returned. Flocco followed this courfe, and arrived at land. This navigator acquired, from this meafure, perhaps a novelty to the people of the Orcades, the furname of Raf'na-Flocco. This ufe of the pilot-raven, common to the Danes and navigators

gators from the Baltic, gives the reafon of their taking the raven for their ftandard.

There is another ftory of one of thefe adventurers, who, when out at fea, in the German ocean, and off the Englifh coaft, let fly a hawk, who made directly for the land, either Suffolk or Norfolk, as now called. This navigator. fteered after this his pilot, his courfe, and fell in with the land. He pretended only to follow his hawk, and to recover it; but his real defign was to fpy the land.

The apologue of the Argonautic expedition, under reference to this ufe made of the flight of birds, relates the circumftance of the pilot of the Argonauts fending off a dove to precede the Argos, on a trial of the paffage through the Straights of the Cyanian Rocks. Lib. ii. p. 563.

The narrative (whether in apologue or fact) of a fimilar tranfaction, hath the fame reference. Noah let fly from the ark a raven and two doves, on an experiment of exploring land, and formed his judgement on the iffue of the experiment.

Thefe

Thefe correfponding narratives are fomething more than curious.

However accounts in the earlieft periods inform us that the navigators of long voyages fteered by obfervation alfo of the *fun* and the *ftar* ; the *load-ftar*.

In the early defective ftate of civil government, which went merely to the œconomical regulations of the family, or hord, thefe adventurers acted upon their own authority : and the *Vic*, or War-captain, was fupreme, each over their own refpective bands : the command was abfolute as a military power ; and when they took poft on any ftation, or finally fettled on any eftablifhed dwelling, they continued, as ftill under military organization, this command.

This the antiquary may fuppofe, and I believe will find, was the origin of Clanfhip and * Taniftry, and of the defpotic fpirit of thefe modes of government, if they could be fo called.

Thefe fea-rovers affumed the appellative Vic, or Vig, as a war name ; as alfo, in a body, that of Viks, Vigs, Viggands, Vi-

* That is, the government of the Tanes, or Thanes, as herein after explained.

kingers,

kingers, and Vicanders, tranfcribed by the Latin writers varioufly, and tranflated Piratæ. Thofe who have read the *Trea-tife on the Mode* of ftudying Antiquities, to which this is a fecond part, referring themfelves to the appendix, No. I. will fee there defcribed, and explained, the diftinctive power in found of the Glôtalls K, G, and Y, or open G*, [Ɏ open, ɏ fhut and afperated as our common vulgate g] as alfo of the labials P, B, V, F, and their interchangeable ufe : He will there fee the nature and application of the digammas; firft, the guttural catch; alfo fecondly, the afperate furcharge; and will very readily conceive how the various manners, in which this word hath by divers people been pronounced and written, might take place, namely, Vic, Vig, Wig, Pic, Vict †,

---

* Olaus Wormius, in the fixth book of his Danifh. Momuments, gives a fragment of an infcription (Infcrip. vi) that hath this word fo written on it, ' *Lapidem hanc pofuit Pic.*'

† Getæ omnes Baiiftanii et Schytæ funt peritiffimi, area fimul et tormenvis ; fed Cimbrici *Ficti* funt hafta gladio et vinulicis fpigis bellum fortiter cientes. E cum legimus diverfas hiftorias, migrationes etiam gentium antiquas confideramus, hinc prodiiffe *Pictos* et *Fictos* qui Athletæ et digladiatores appellantur.

Lyfeandri Antiq. Dan. Sermone 3tio.

This quotation fhews that the word *Pict* was an appellative and war name, although it does not give the true derivation.

D   Pict,

Fict, Pict, Peaght, Petæ, Vita, * Wight. Under all thefe names are thefe fea-rovers found mentioned. Be it here remarked and remembered, that this word was originally only an appellative, and no more the name of a people or nation than the word Pirata. After · they became fettled, this, under moft of its variations, and with its various compounds, 'might and did become the *name* of a people ; as Picti, Pictones, Viccingi, Vectæ, Vectones, Victores, Vettæ, Vettones, Viccingi, Victuriones.

This word alfo fometimes fimply, at other times in the compound, becomes an appellative, or cognomen, to feveral of their leaders, even to one of their kings. Froto fecundus cognomine Vig-etus. Vitto Frifiorum pirata; alfo Vict-red, Viglet, Guit-lac, Vit or Wit-lac, Viggo, and others of the like import. From this fame Cymric or Cimbric root comes alfo Viigur, the adjective *fortis* ; alfo the Teu-

---

* Thus, while at this day the North-Britons pronounce the word *eight* (octo) with the g fhut and afperated, the South-Britons pronounce it with the open g or y, as *eyht*; fo the word *Wight*, and *Vect*, or *Veght*, is pronounced Wiyht ; and Vita, as alfo *Peta*, by different authors ; and even fometimes thus differently by the fame author.

tifch, or Saxon, compound Wig-huis, a
ftrong houfe or caftle, and Wig-ftow, a
camp.

This word Vic, in its radical and prime
fignification, was not unknown in the
Latin language : it is found even in Virgil. Æn. II. p. 433.

> Teftor in occafu veftro, nec tela, nec ullas
> Vitaviffe *vices* Danaum.

Which word Servius in his Commentary
explains, *pugnas* et Ifidorus narrat *vicam*
dixiffe pro victoriam. That fome word
fignifying the fame thing, and derived
from the fame root, was not unknown to
Tacitus, although now loft out of the text,
appears more than probable.

In giving an account [de moribus Germ.
§ 2.] of the origin of the appellative *Ger-*
manus, he fays it was an appellative or
title lately affumed. Ita nationis nomen
non gentis evaluiffe paulatim. Ut omnes
primò [ ] *a victore* ob metum, mox à
feipfo invento nomine, Germani vocarentur. All the commentators allow this
paffage, as it ftands now in the text, to
be very defective, and not very intelligible ; and they make various unfuccefsful
attempts to explain it ; fome have cor-

rected

rected **Victore** for **Victis**. Now it appears to me that if the critic will put the word Vic, or Vict, in the place where I have put the crotchets, the appellative by which they were known to the Gauls, when firſt they croſſed the Rhine, the paſſage will not only be plainly intelligible, but will give the account, in fact, of theſe people, thus, " Ut omnes primùm [*Victi* or *Vigti*] *a victore* (or as it is in ſome MSS *victis*) ob metum, mox a ſeipſo invento nomine Germani vocarentur. They were at firſt, through fear, called victs, or pirates; afterwards theſe people aſſumed a more honourable name of themſelves, and were called Germans, that is *Warr-men*, or warriours. The Gauls, or Celts, (if you pleaſe, as they were in the moſt early times) had been uſed to ſuffer by the incurſions of the *Vics*, it was therefore natural from the impreſſion which theſe invaders excited, when they croſſed the Rhine, that the inhabitants ſhould call them *Vics* or *Victs*, Piratæ.

When the communities of theſe nations were organized in the form of civil government; and whole countries became kingdoms under a ſovereign power; the kingdoms ſent out ſuch parties of Pirates,

or

or Vicanders. Thefe commanders being no longer independent, but acting under a delegated power, then firft (as I think I can difcover, took the title of *Degans*, or *Thag'ns*, pronounced by us Thanes, and Danes, fignifying a leader, as may be feen repeatedly on the Runic ftones. Thefe kings ufed to fend out their beft warriours, and frequently their fons, either to make eftablifhments, or to reconnoitre and prepare for fuch, in foreign parts. Whenever thefe Thegans, or Dhagens, made their eftablifhments, and fettled, they continued the fame command, as under the fame delegated authority, and affumed a title which the Latin writers of their hiftory tranflated *Reguli*; hence the multiplicity of kings which we read of, at thefe times, in fo many different places. The conftitution (if fuch may be called a conftitution) of thefe petty clans of colonies, was called Thanelagen, by a name which is continued, in Ireland to this day, in the word *Tanifry*.

Before this effay proceeds in its attempt to trace the very interefting hiftory of thefe fea-rovers called Ficts, by the Welfh the *Fictiad*, and Picts, a people fo little underftood; we will, if the reader pleafes,

recur

recur back to an enquiry after the inhabitants of Britain, originally as well as primarily adventitious, upon whom thefe fea-rovers made their incurfions, and amongft whofe borders they afterward fettled.

The Cymric tribes, · called Cimbri, dwelling on the fea, became naturally, as well as of neceffity, a marine people and navigators. The antiquary will find them in the earlieft ages of the world's inhabitancy, paffed over to Britain, and dwelling there. Tribes of the Teutifch race, the Folc, Volc, or Bolg, pronounced by the Romans Belgæ; paffed alfo over from the lower parts of Gaul to the Southern parts of Brittain (fome fay from Spain alfo, to Ireland) in the very firft ages. Thefe emigrations of Cymric and Teutifch tribes differing *at firft* in their language, merely as by a dialect of the fame, and coming in very different directions, were the firft known inhabitants of this our ifland, fo as to have been confidered as the Indigenæ *.

Speaking in the next place of the adventitious inhabitants who came hither,

* Brittones olim impleverunt Brittaniam et judicaverunt à mari ad mare, id eft, à Totenefs ad Cattenefs.

Nennius, c. 3.

after

after thefe primary inhabitants were fettled, I fhall mention firft, though the
lateft *longo intervallo*, the Vir-bolg or Belgæ, Teutifch tribes, become, by long fe-
paration, totally different from the Cymric. Thefe paffed over into Britain about
60 or 70 years before the time of Julius
Cæfar, and poffeffed the South-eaftern and
Southern parts of the ifland, and pent up
the Cymri, in Cornwall, that is to fay, in
Devon and Cornwall, the Irifh remaining at that time undifturbed, by whom-
foever it was inhabited.

This fact then thus fettled out of our
way, fo as to have no occafion to recur
again to it, we will commence our inquiry
after the *earlieft adventitious* inhabitants, by
reftating that this ifland was poffeffed by
the Cymric and Dteufch tribes, under the
common name of Britons, as the firft inhabitants. Now thofe tribes of the Teutifch, called Belgæ, which we have before
feen, dwelt on the Southern coafts of the
Baltic, and who, as deriving their generation from *Gott-teus*, took the patronymic
appellation *Cotti, Gotti, Gothi, or Codi
(from

---

* There are accounts in the Gothland Antiquities of a
migration of thefe people, occafioned by the increafe of population exceeding the difproportion of the fupply. One
third part were deftined to emigrate; and a Thegan, or
leader, was appointed to conduct and command them :

they

(from whofe name the Baltic was called Sinus Codanus, or Cottanus) may be confidered as the firft *adventitious fettlers* in Britain. Thefe advancing in the proceffion of their generations and habitancy in the rear, and upon the flanks of the Cymri, in the fame manner as they had done upon the Continent, having become, in the procefs of time, marine navigators alfo, followed the Cymri into the Orcades, the Northern parts of Scotland, the Weftern ifles, and at length into Ireland and Britain. The reader will obferve, that this effay is here fpeaking of the early migrations by which thefe almoft Weftern parts of Europe became inhabited, not of the piratical incurfions of the Pics or Vics, of much later date. Ammianus Marcellinüs informs us [Lib. xxvii. c. 8.] that the Atta-Cotti, Bellicofiffima Gens, and [Es-Cotti] 'Scotti were found there *. Nennius relates, as an

---

they refifted at firft, and their leader was killed. Helguo, a fecond leader, was appointed ; they migrated by fea in a great fleet of fhips. Vide Nicol. Petreus. Lyfchander and Olaus Wormius. This migration is by the Gothic and Danifh chronologifts, placed A. M. 2500.

* Britto es venerunt in tertiâ ætate mundi ad Britraniam, Scytl æ autem (id eft (1) Scotti) in quarta ætate mundi obtinueru..t Hiberniam.   Nennius.

(1) The Cambro-Brittons, fays Mr. Carte, called them Ys Cotti.

. hiftoric

hiſtoric faɛt, what this eſſay ſtates only as a
conjeɛture, the order and ſucceſſion of the
emigrations of the Cymric tribes, called,
when ſettled, Britons, and of the Teutiſch
adventitious inhabitants called 'Scotti.
*Tacitus alſo informs us that the Æſtui, one
of theſe Baltic tribes, ſpoke the ſame language as the Britons ; ✝ and that the red
hair, and frame of body of the Britons,
beſpoke them as being of this Teutiſch
race. This eſſay will therefore venture to
ſtate the 'Scotti as emigrants, from the
Cotti, (afterwards called Gothi, who poſſeſſed the coaſts of the Baltic,) and therefore called Atta-Cotti, *progenies Cottica*, a
word compounded of the generical name
Cottus, and *Ætte*, written on the Runic
monuments *Etiar*, progenies, familia, or
race, ‡ the Ys-Cotti or Es-Cotti, pronounced 'Scotti, a word, which when the
prefix Es is added to it, means the re-

---

* Dextro Suevici maris littore æſluorum gentes alluun-
tur, quibus ritus habituſque Suevorum, lingua Brittanicæ
propior.   Tacitus de Mor. Germ. § 45.
✝ Cæterùm Brittaniam qui mortales initio coluerunt indigenæ an advecti, ut inter barbaros parum compertum.
Habitus corporum varii atque ex eo argumenta. Namque
rutilæ Calidoniam habitantium comæ, magnique artus
Germanicam originem aſſeverunt.
            Tacit. de Vita Agricolæ, § 11.
‡ ————————— *in remotiſſimis* Scotiæ finibus.
                        Saxo Gram.

mote,

mote, utmoſt, or external, Cotti, dwelling
beyond, or over the mountains, or other
relative boundary ; and meant here, particularly the Cotti, who dwelt in the Orcades, in *Cat*-neſs and Strathnarvern,
* on the other ſide, or over the Highlands ;
as alſo the Weſtern Cotti †, whether in
Hibernia or Calidonia.

Hiſtory gives us an account of one '*Scot-
tus*, a friend and brother-in-law of Frotho,
the firſt king of the Danes, living in theſe
parts, as the remoteſt parts—*qui et ipſe
Scottici nominis conditor fuit*. I quote this,
not as coinciding with my opinion of the
faét, for I am convinced the name is of
much earlier date, but ſimply to ſtate that
the Cotti were in theſe remote parts called

---

* In remotiſſimis Scotiæ finibus. Saxo Gramm.
† I do not here enter into the difpute, in which the
Scots and Iriſh are engaged, whether the 'Scots paſſed
from Ireland to Scotland, or from Scotland to Ireland : both
theſe people, the Calidonian and Iriſh Scotti, came from
the Cotti of the Baltic, and were both adventitious. I am
not ignorant of the traditionary ſtory of the emigrants, ſuppoſed to have come from Spain to Ireland, and to have
ſettled in the Southern parts of it. That ſuch, if any
ſuch thus emigrated, were *Celts*, might eaſily be proved ;
but when the ancient Iriſh hiſtorians call them 'Scotti, (if
they mean more by that word than the general appellative
Scythians) I cannot but think that they have been inadver-
tently led to confound them with the Cotti, who came from
the Baltic, and ſettled in the *Northern* parts of Ireland.

Yͤs,

Ys, or Es-Cotti, pronounced 'Scotti, at this time near 700 years before Chrift.

Having thus endeavoured to ftate the proceffions and fucceffion of migrations to, and the inhabitancy of, the Britifh ifles, the effay now returns to its endeavour to form fome account of the fea-rovers of the Northern parts of Europe, who, in procefs of time, became A VERY GREAT NAVAL POWER.

The ancient ftone monuments, in the Runic infcriptions, on which the names of feveral of thefe Vics and Dag'ns, or Thag'ns, remain; and on fome of which* their actions are recorded, are living tefti-monies, that fuch men and fuch things were. Many of the actions of individuals, and tranfactions of the people, are related in the ancient poems; thefe are mixed, no doubt, with fable, but founded on truth. The Antiquary knows that it was part of the civil inftitution of thefe people to record and tranfmit their hiftory in the *Viifur* of the Scaldri; and that it was part of the pomp and circumftance of their war to have fome of thefe recording

* For inftance that they made their incurfions on Bri-tain, alfo on Aquitain.

poets

poets in their suite. From thefe monumental records and traditionary poems, their earlieft hiftorians derived their facts : and the commentaries of their moft learned antiquaries have drawn forth thefe teftimonies into proof. This, furely, is as good, if not better, ground of evidence than any from which the Greek or Roman hiftorians derived the accounts which they give of the early fabulous periods ; and perhaps one may add, of fome of thofe early times which they give as hiftoric. Thefe accounts are difcredited by their own writers : and therefore, feparating fable from fact, I never hefitated to give a preference of credit to thefe Northern hiftories beyond what I can give to the ftory of Æneas, being the founder of the Roman nation, &c. &c.

The Cymric tribes having become by their maritime fituation in an ifland, the ifland of Scandinavia, marine navigators, foon began to exercife the power which this gave them, as Sea-rovers, Vics, Vigs, Viggands, &c. And thus * this people, who

* Hablingus, Varnlingi filius Gothlandiæ præfes,
Celebris fuit octavus Cimbrorum judex nomine Ingwarus.   Gothic Annales.
Hunguarus frater Hablingi, Gothlandiæ principis, et Gunderus, germanus Inguari propè Slefvicam navali prælio

who had been at land, and on the Continent, always inferior to, and repreſſed by
the Teutiſch tribes, under this form of
power in their turn, recoiled upon the
Teuts; made incurſions upon them;
fixed ſtations in their maritime borders,
ſo as to make eſtabliſhments in Gothland,
and on the Saxon ſhores. They became,
even in the earlieſt ages, an aſcendant *naval
power* in the Baltic, not then a Mediterranean ſea; ſo as that, when the Teutones and
'Saxones firſt commenced *their* naval courſes
in this way of ſea-rovers *, theſe Cymric Vics ſettled in Gothland, repreſſed and
reſtrained their piracies; they not only
repulſed them from the ſea, but at
times held them ſubdued at land, and governed them, eſpecially the Angles and

lio vicerunt Helmilconem fortiſſimum piratarum Theuto-
niæ et Slaviæ.
   N. B. J. Suaning quotes this from C. Lyſcander, and
places it in his Chronology in the year 1547, before Chriſt.

   * Hablingus dux Gothlandiæ ad Theutones (qui tum
primùm piraticam exercebant) cum inſtructa claſſe emiſit
fratrem Hunguarum. Is, aſſumptis in ſocietatem belli et
periculorum germanis ſuis Gerardo et Berchone, piratas
inſulis Carolinis ejecit; et navali pugnâ attritis hoſtiles eorum depredationes fortiſſimè repreſſit.
   J. Suaning ſays, that the Gothic Annales place this fact
in the year of the world 2394; but, quoting Claud. Lyſcan-
cer, he places it in the year 2420, and before Chriſt 1523.

'Saxones,

'Saxones, by Reguli or tributary kings, called Scots-conung : I have faid, *at times*, for there were various fluxes and refluxes of the tide of conqueft amongft thefe people, the Teutones, Angles, or 'Saxones, oftentimes making inroads, and fometimes even conquefts on the Cimbric Cherfoneffus *. Finally, however, the Cimbri fettled, as I have faid, in Gothland, and on the Saxon fhores, where hiftory finds them under the name Secambri †. To give, *feriatim*, an account of thefe fea-rovers, of their prædatory expeditions, of their invafions, fettlements, and conquefts, would be writing the hiftory of the firft ages of thefe tribes and nations; for, by thefe War-captains, thefe Vics, and their Vicanders, as independant bands, were the firft fettlements and conquefts made. But, howfoever indepen-

---

* Manifeftum autem in fermonibus expeditionum fiat, omnes aquilonares gentes, et præcipuè eas quæ Cherfoneffum inhabitant, ad quas iter terreftre patet, incitatas bello occupaffe vicina maritima ab Ablo ad Viftulam.
Ubi et verfus ulteriora Tuifconitarum, ferè omnes gentes invenimus, quas jam in Cimbria recenfuimus.
C. Lyfcander, apud Olaum Wormium, lib. v.
Eundem Germaniæ *finum* Cimbri *proximi oceano* tenent.
Tacit. de Mor. Germ. § 37.

† Some of thefe tribes were, from their fituation, called Sicambri, as Rudbec fays, Zee-cimbri.
Strabo et Plinius.

dent

dent thefe firft adventurers were in their
excurfions and in their fettlements, when
the nation, whence they came, had in
procefs of time acquired the unity, organization, and ftrength of government,
the Imperium of that government, not
only fent forth, as I have ftated Dag'ns,
or Thagn's, with delegated power to make
foreign fettlements ; but reduced moft of
the independant fettlements of the Vics to
fubjection under this power: either appointing Reguli over them, or making the
actual exifting ruler a tributary Scots-Co-
ning. They called thefe fettlements by a
name which anfwers to the modern idea of
colony or province, Thag'n-lands ; whilft
the Thag'ns paid Dag'n, or Thag'n-geld,
or Scot ; as the fyftem of law by which
they were governed was called Thag'n-
legen, whence the power of the Lairds of
Clans, and that relict of obfolete power
called in Ireland *Taniftry.*

The Vics, Pics, Vicingers, &c. were,
at firft, as it feems to me, private * and in-
depen-

* Wherever thefe adventurers fucceeded, and carried
their meafures to the point of making eftablifhed fettlements, they held the government of the Civil State (if that
ftate could be called civil) as well as the command of the
military : hence it is we find in the hiftory of thefe people fuch a multitude of kings (I do not mean here *reguli* or
viceroys)

dependent fea-rovers; although I think this appellative was afterwards ufed as the name of an office, fimilar to what we now call admiral.

The appellative Deg'n, or Theg'n, had generally reference to community and government, as holding *delegated* power under, or connected with, fovereign power; but neither was this always fo at firft, for it fignified fimply a leader, as may be feen in the Scolingen infcription, *Herden Guden Diag'n,* which is literally exercitûs bonus *Dux.* This word, through the general indecifion of fpelling, and the promifcuous ufe of the letters of the fame organ, has been written Dia-g-n, De-g-n, Dey-n, The-g-n, The-y-n, Dane, and in Latin Thanus, Dainus, T'anus, D'anus. By putting together all that one reads of this word in Olaus Wormius, and Ihre's Gloffary, it appears that it originally meant a military man; next, *per excellentiam,* a commander, and finally *comes regni,* or a

viceroys) in one tract of country. Thirty of thefe kings, fequebantur Frothonem qui ipfum amicitiâ aut obfequio colerent. And again—Eo bello 170 reges qui aut ex Hunnis erant, aut inter Hunnos militaverant fubmifère fe regi.

Saxo Gramm. Lib. v. p. 89.

Harald Hyldetand 70 *reges maritimos* nauticarum virium certamine confumpfit.   .   Id. lib. viii.

count,

Count, or a Governor of a Province, either by office or tenure. Another diſtinction between theſe two words occurs to me, that Vic and Vickin applies rather to a ſea-command : and Tha-g-n, Tha-y-n, and Dane, to a command at land. Both at times will be found, in the hiſtory of theſe people, applied to ſelf-created commands ; and both alſo again to official commands, when the power of the nation concentred into government. It will alſo be found, that both from *appellative titles* were, in the courſe of events, aſſumed as *national names.* Hence the *appellative* Vic, or Pict, became the *national name* of the Picts, when ſettled as a nation, in Scotland ; and of Pictones and Victones in Poitou, and Vettones in Spain. This firſt name ſeems to have taken place in the ſettlements made under their marine power : and the latter name of Danes, when the Thegns of the Cimbri and Goths choſe one ſupreme Thane, in Latin Danus. This was the firſt monarch of the people, who hence after took the national name of Danes. This fact is pre-ciſely and ſpecifically related by Saxo Gram-maticus.

E   The

The Cimbri Cotti, and other people of the Baltic, had communications, and alliances, and wars, with the Britifh Ifles in the very earlieft times. They were great navigators ; and Britain, under their ftate of navigation, was reckoned to be only feven days fail from their ports. How they fet, and kept their courfe, out at fea, is explained in another part of this treatife. The hiftory of thefe people gives accounts of the incurfions which they made upon, and the fettlements which they made in, the Orcades, the Weftern Ifles, Scotland, and Ireland, from 800 years before the Chriftian æra to 1000 years after it.

The Vics*, or Pics, were the firft private adventurers, and took that appellative as a national name when they fettled in Scotland. When they were fpoken of in the community, or as a body, they were called the *Vic-* or *Pic-Thiód*, from the word *Thiód*, ufed commonly in the compounds, and fignifying *populus, com--munitas.* The Welfh, by changing P

---

* Johannis Fordune, in his Hiftory of the Scots (chap. 5.) defcribes *Scythia Inferior*, and fays, " habet ab oriente mare Mediterraneum, quod ibidem Balticum dicitur, a Bath loco ubi terram intrat ab Oceano, à qua regione fecundum quofdam Albigenfes, Pidti, progreffi funt.

into

into Ph, or F, called them *Fictiad*. The Romans, many ages after, when they had occafions to know them by their incurfions, called them Picti, and Pictones, Victi, Victiones, and Vetiones. The Latin writers of the Britifh Hiftory (as Cambden fays) called them Viccingi. The Teuts and Saxons pronounced this name by diffolving the harfh guttural into the open one, and called them Peayhtæ, Petæ, and Vitæ.

Bede fays *, and fays very truly, that the Picts came in long fhips, from Scythia (meaning Scandinavia †.) The appellative, Scyths, was no longer applied to the Teutifch race, who, in his time were called Germans, in general ; but, at the fame time, the feveral people by their diftinctive names. Scyth was only applied

---

* Contigit gentem Pictorum de Scythia, ut perhibent, longis navibus non multis Oceanum ingreffum.
 Bedæ Hift. Eccl. Angliæ. L. 1. c. 1.
 Inde Scotiæ & Petiæ, infularumque quas Auftrales et Meridionales vocant. Saxo Gram. Lib. 9, p. 171.
 Picti venerunt et occupaverunt infulas quæ Orcades vocantur. Nennius Hift. Brit. c. 5.
 Picti habitare per Septentrionales infulæ partes cœperunt. Beda ut fupra.
 † Scytharum nomen ufquequaque tranfit in Sarmatos et Germanos : nec aliis prifca illa appellatio quam qui extremi gentium harum, ignoti prope cæteris mortalibus degunt.
 Plinii Nat. Hift. Lib. 4. c. 12.

to thofe who, beyond the hiftoric horizon, were scarcely known to the civilized world. Nennius fays, they firft seized the Orcades; and, Bede adds, afterwards the northern parts of Britain.

That thefe Picts came at firft as fea-rovers, and PIRATES, in their character of Vics and Vickanders, not as emigrating colonies, appears from their* company confifting only of men. When they took up the idea of fettling, they obtained wives of the Scots *on this condition*, that, whenever there fhould arife a doubt as to the fucceffion to the crown, they fhould chofe their King (for, almoft all Kings were then elective) from the female rather than the male line; which cuftom remained, as Bede fays, to his time. This explains the reafon and original caufe of the government of the Picts falling finally into that of the Scots.

The Scotti being in fettled poffeffion of the northern parts of Ireland, at the time

---

* Uxores Picti non habentes peterunt à 'Scotis eâ folâ conditione, ut ubi res veneret in dubium, magis de fœmineâ regum profapia, quam de mafculina, regem fibi eligerent. Quod ufque hodiè apud Pictos conftat efle fervatum.

Bedæ Hift. Eccl. Angliæ. Lib 1. c. 1.

Hermathruda fœmina regnavit in 'Scotia; which is placed about 430 years before Chrift.

Saxo Gramm. Lib. 3. p. 57.

that

that thefe Vickanders, Viks, Piks, or
Piƈts, came, refifted their attempts upon
that Ifland, but affifted then by their
advice ; and *, as fhould appear, by other
means, to make their incurfions upon the
northern parts of Britain. Thefe people
were never, in their charaƈter of fea-rovers,
or *Piƈts*, in poffeffion of any part of
Ireland. Although afterwards, as *Thag'ns*†,
they made perpetual incurfions upon it,
and had various conneƈtions and alliances
with it. The firft of thefe who came to
Ireland, are faid, by the Irifh Hiftory, to
come from the country *Fomoire*, which is
juft the very place whence the Cotti came.
Pœmore, or Fœmore, means marfhy
and fenny lands, and part of that country
retains to this day this name, Pœmore-ania‡.
When afterwards the Thagns from the

* 'Scoti remiferunt Piƈtos ad feptentrionales partes Bri-
taniæ, opem contra Brittonas adverfantes, fi infurgerent,
promittentes. Ranulph Higden, Lib. 1.
    I refer the word 'Scoti here to the Irifh—the reader will
refer it as he pleafes.
    † I affume an authority for writing the name in this
manner; firft, as I find it fo written of old in their own
monuments; and next, as they themfelves called the ifland
Thanet, or Little Dania.
    ‡ Mor, Moer, Moor——Terra paluftris, inde eft quod
Pomerania Sclavonice diƈta fit *Pomores*, à *po*, apud, et mor.
—Flandri ex eâdem caufâ Morini olim appellati. Ihres's
Sueio-Gothic Gloffary.

E 3   Cymbric

Cymbric Scandinavia had connections in Ireland, we hear of the later name *Lock-Lyun*, or the Island in the Lake.

These Viks, Piks, or Piks, under the name of Vittæ, or Vitæ*, which name they were called by, on the Saxon shore, poſſeſſed the the maritime parts of Kent, and the Iſle of *Wight*, called Vectæ, Vita, Vicht, Wight, Wiyt, &c. alſo Petia.

The Reader will not expect, notwithſtanding what Cambden is inclined to think, and what Innes has undertaken to prove; notwithſtanding what Auſonius, Claudian, and Iſidorus ſay; that we ſhould now enter into the diſproving that ſilly opinion of the Piks being ſo called from their *Tattooing* their bodies. Almoſt all uncivilized and half-cloathed people have always done, and do ſtill, the ſame. It was not peculiar to theſe people, as a race: the Britons ſhould rather have had this appellative even though their language differed in dialect, both from the Britons and Scots, ſo far removed, as in time to

---

* Strabo, ſpeaking of the Ἰάποδες. Lib. 7. p. 315. ſays, κατάριχλοι [that is, literally, tattoed] δ'ὁμοίως τοῖς ἄλλοις Ἰλλυρίοις κ, Θρᾳξί.

become

become even a different language *. In the time of Bede it was become neceſſary to have five different tranſlations of the Scriptures for the uſe of the inhabitants of Britain, viz. Britiſh, Engliſh, Scottiſh, Pickiſh, and Latin.

Theſe Viks, Piks, Vikins, or Vikingers, ſtopt not their courſes in Britain, but puſhed forward their expeditions along the coaſts, on both ſides the Channel. They could never make any permanent impréſſions on the Belgic coaſts, or, if they were on thoſe coaſts before the Belgæ arrived, they were ouſted thence. There were in the Roman times no traces of them there, the † Victores excepted. They are, however, found ſeparate on the Coaſts of Normandy, under Cimbric and Suïo-gothic names; as ‡ Ambibares, Ambialites; and on the Coaſts of Lower

* Hæc {ſcil. Britania] in preſenti, juxta numerum librorum quibus Lex divina ſcripta eſt, quinque gentium linguis unam eandemque ſummæ veritatis & veræ ſublimitatis ſcientiam ſcrutatur & confitetur; Anglorum, videlicet, Brittonum, Scottorum, Pictorum, & Latinorum, quæ meditatione ſcripturarum cæteris omnibus eſt facta communis. Bedæ Hiſt. Eccle. L. 1. c. 1.

† Unde cum conſecuti Batavi veniſſent, & Heruli, Joviique & *Victores*. Amm. Marcell. Lib. 27. c. 28.

‡ This is the name of a maritime, or naval, diſtrict, in the military diviſion of a country. Ham ſignifies a certain quota of naval regiſtered ſeamen (Ihre's Gloſſary) to be ſupplied by a certain diſtrict. Hence we find the Ambivari in the lower marine diſtrict of the Sceld.

Brittany,

Brittany, as a separate maritime people, by the names of Diablintes * and Venetæ †. They are found settled in the regions of the Loire, under the names Pict-ones, which means *settled Piats* : and, in general, on the Coasts of the Oceanus Aquitanicus, even in Spain under the appellative Vett-ones and Vectones ‡.

I have dared to assert that, that race of people, called Κυνή]ας, from the Celtic word *Cynhaith*, who possessed the Western coasts of Europe, as mentioned by Herodo-tus, were some of those very sea-rovers; for, there are many reasons sufficient to state it as a conjecture, not unworthy the research of the antiquary. These Kuneetæ were certainly different from the Gallic Celts, in person, language, and manners : these did not advance over land before them ; and must therefore have come by sea ; they were equally different from the Belgæ : what therefore could they be but these Baltic sea-rovers. The very name given to the countries, wherein they set-

---

* Diablin is the same name, and of the same import, as Diaflyn, the name which they gave to the post of Dublin, in Ireland.

† Ven-aittæ means the tribes of Fenmen.

‡ Lucan, lib. 4. ↓ 8.

tled,

tled, marks that the fettlements were made by colonifts, or tribes, of thefe peo‑ ple. The country of the Loire, which was fettled by thefe, was called *Pictavia*. *Ach-y-Thegn* feems to be no unfair or much ftrained etymology of Ακουϊταν, and exprefles, that it was the country poffeffed by *Tribes of Tanes*, or Danes.

Fact moreover confirms this conjecture *, The old Runic monuments, and the annals of thefe very people mention their expedi‑ tions and incurfions into thefe countries †.

Fordun

---

* Ex hoc Hyperboreorum campo ingenti numero regum filii, ac Martis focii aufpiciifque Neptuni militia tum in orbem prodierunt. Hifpaniam regnaque alia devicârunt quarum rerum geftarum memoriam annales noftri Lapidei Cippi hic delineati ab oblivione temporumque injuriâ vin‑ dicant. Perifkioldi Monumenta Sueio-Gothica. Lib. 1. c. 1. In the firft fection of the third chapter, he gives a draw‑ ing of a monument of Sigvid, who was a great invader of England. In the courfe of defcribing which, he fays, " Hujus exempla complura occurrunt." And, after men‑ tioning feveral infcriptions, each recording the expeditions of the perfon, to whom the Runic infcription is erected, he goes on——& complurium qui occidentales regiones, Hif‑ paniafque ac loca extera inviferant mentionem faciunt Cippi noftri lapidei, quorum nos fuo ordine, defcriptionem daturi erimus: fimulque oftendemus titulos hos infignes, vel ideo datos, fuiffe, quod vel exercitus duces olim, vel militiæ Socii fuerunt. Tales numero plures originis Gothicæ illuf‑ tres viros quondam agnoverat Anglia, ipfaque Hibernia, qui ante complura fecuta ifto in orbe mortui fuit. Idem.

† In his diebus, fcilicet Romanæ captivitatis, de Pictavia progreffi cum fua familia Picti trans fretum Brittanicum setibus Hiberniam adibant. Fordune, Scot. Hift. c. 4.

Populus

Fordun takes up the matter of fact as a matter of notoriety, that the Picts did possess Poictou and Aquitain. The only difference between the chronicles, and those who write from, and reason upon them, is, whether they came thence, and made their incursions upon Britain; or whether they went out from Britain, and hence made their incursions into Gaul. *That they were there is the ground and fact.* That they came from Scythia to these countries is the opinion that Fordun, with the authority of Bede, seems to abide by. This account of the inhabitants of Acquitania, seems to me the only probable one, by which the description of Kuneetæ, given by Herodotus, and the description of Gaul, given by Cæsar, Strabo †, and others, as inhabited by three different race of people, can be explained.

Populus quidam ignotus ab Aquitaniæ finibus emergens. Qui *postea* Pictus dicebatur suo scilicet Albaniæ littori ratibus applicuit. Pictorum autem accessus ad hanc insulam (scil. Brittaniam) per varios variè describitur Auctores. Quorum quidem tradunt, quod a gentibus quas secum *ex Scythia* Rex Humber ad Brittaniam condux erat.— Alia Chronica. Picti quidem exorti de Scythia, fugam Agenoris comitati sunt, &, ipso dvce, insiderunt Aquitanorum nationem in quâ Picti de proprio nomine Pictaviam condiderunt. Id. c. 29.

† Ακουϊτανοὶ διαφέροισι τῷ Γαλατικῷ φύλῳ καλά τε τὰς τῶν σωμάτων καλασκιυὰς, κ̀ καλὰ τὴν γλῶτlαν.

Strabo, Lib. 4. p. 189.

This

This alfo accounts for the nature of the irruptions made by the remote nations coming from the extreme northern ocean upon Italy and Rome itfelf. This was an entrepôt, an intermediate poft; and they had water-carriage up to the heads of the Loire *, and Garone, which interlock with the waters of the Rhone and Mediterranean. † This was a trading rout perfectly known to the Romans, and to thefe people.

Thefe fea-rovers purfued their prædatory enterprizes, each Vik, Vikin, or Vikinger, with one feparate band, and in his own fleet, Numbers, however, of thefe fometimes joined in thefe expeditions. At length there were two inftances of their forming communities, or civil bodies, of pirates, not unlike what the government of Rome was at its firft eftablifhment. The Jomfberg-Vikingers, who took poft and built a ftrong city on the Ifland Julin, or Wollin, was one inftance. Thefe main-

---

* The Senones, the fettled inhabitants of the Seine, one of the tribes who facked Rome. L. Florus, Lib. 1. c. 15. fays of thefe, " Hi *quondam* ab ultimis terrarum oris, et cingente omnia Oceano, ingenti agmine profecti.

† Vide Strabo, Lib. 4. p. 189, who defcribes particularly this rout in its navigable parts, and the portages over land, from one fet of waters to the other.

tained

tained an independent fovereign ftation, and had for fome time an afcendant naval power in thofe feas. The antiquary will meet with matter of much curiofity in their hiftory. The Rofcheild Vikingers were another inftance, but of another kind, not fo independent; an eftablifh-ment fomething like our Cinque Ports.

From thefe beginnings *the Keel of a great naval power and dominion was laid*, which, by degrees, was built up to that magnitude and force, which commanded all the north of Europe, and finally be-came fuperior to, and afcendent over, even the Roman Empire itfelf.

If the antiquary will be fo good as to attend to the few traces of the progreffive growth of this great northern maritime power, he will fee that it was but natural that fuch a hardy, ftrong, fierce, warlike, race, continually habituated to danger and trained to war, fhould finally form a great naval dominion; and, by the operations of its fleets, be enabled to advance in force upon all the coafts of Europe; and, alfo, up the rivers, into the very heart of it : he will fee, that it was in the ordinary courfe of human events, that this power fhould,

as

as it did, become fuperior at fea ; equal at land, and, finally, fuperior at land alfo, to the power of Rome.

There * are many curious anecdotes of the naval enterprizes of thofe northern naval people many hundred years before the æra of the building of Rome †, and many inftances of foreign excurfions undertaken, and fettlements made, in foreign parts, by them.

This treatife, however, will commence its review, only about the time of the building of Rome, when thefe people by various alliances of marriage, and politics; and by various conquefts, had concentred

---

* Danis paritèr atq; Norwagis hôc in more pofitum antiquitùs comperimus. Quod frequentes fufceperent, non in vicinas tantùm, fed etiam remotiffimas terras, expeditiones. Quod inde (ut alia nunc taceam) factum eft, quod fæpe copicfam poft fe fobolem relinquerint Reges: de quorum fingulis liberis pro dominandi libidine non fufficere vifa fit patria : alii eorum domi regnum adminiftrarunt: alii claffe ac Commeatu inftructi, *Maris Imperium* ex ufu & commodo fuo gubernandum fibi vindicarunt. Neque etiam dubium ipfos hujus Plagæ Septentrionalis incolas, bellis continuis affuetos, & quafi innutritos, quum domi haud multo pace crefcerent, nec quo Marte clarerent, haberent, foris gloriæ & nominis illuftrandi materiam, bello atque armis quæfiviffe. Andreas Vellerius in Adan. Bremen.

† I have, merely to fketch out fome idea of thefe great leading pirates, given a chronological lift of fome of the principal perfons.

many

many of the nations of the Baltic, into one civil community, and one general empire, under the name of Danes. And were become a great and powerful nation, although yet concealed, as lying beyond the bounds of the *hiſtoric horizon.*

In 762 years before the Chriſtian æra, FROTHO ſucceeded his father Hadingus. He had a great fleet. He ſubdued Scotland, Ireland, Britain, Teuthonia, Slavia, Freſia, and Ruſſia *. He alſo paſſed up the Rhine, and made incurſions upon the extreme borders of Germany.

In 630, Haldane, the ſon of Frotho, died. Upon his death his ſons did, according to what the father had recommended, and according to the ſpirit of the times, divide the empire. Roë, the elder, took the empire of the landed dominions; and Helgo†, the empire of the ſea. Helgo took up the character of a Vik (tranſlated

---

* Rhenum deinde claſſe rimatus extremis Germaniæ partibus manus injecit. Saxo Gramm. Lib. 2. p. 25.
† Diviſo cum fratre imperio Maris poſſeſſionem ſortibus Helgo obtinuit. Regem Sclaviæ Scalcum maritimis copiis laceſſitum oppreſſit. Quam cum in provinciam redigiſſet, varios pelagi receſſus vago navigationis genere perluſtrabat, cum ad inſulam Thoræ reflexiſſet, &c.
Saxo Gramm. Lib. 2. p. 28.

pirate),

pirate), and maintained a great command at sea, and in the maritime parts. At length his brother Roë having been killed by Hotobrode, he returned to Dania ; Hotobrodum quoque cum omnibus copiis navali prælio delevit. And afcended the throne of his father.

About the fifth century before Chrift, in the reign of Roderic Slingebond, the Danes had various connections of alliances and treaties with Britain and Ireland.

About the middle of the fecond century, before the Chriftian Æra, Dan the Third reigned in this great naval kingdom*. He was mafter of a moft immenfe fleet, with which he reduced the Saxons to the condition of becoming tributary.

In this reign, about 100 years before Chrift, the famous Cimbric incurfion into the Roman empire took place.

The reader will remember that we have before remarked, from the hiftory of thefe

* Danorum Juventus Albiam fluvium tantâ navigiorum frequentiâ complevit, ut facile ejus tranfitum proinde ac continuo ponte juncta puppium tabulata præftarent. Quo evenit ut Saxoniæ Rex conditioni tributario adigeretur.

Saxo Gramm. Lib. 4. p. 66.

people,

people, that the Cimbri had settled upon
the Saxon coasts, on the confines of the
Teutones, whom they held under a kind
of subjection, or rather *fœdus inequale*.
He will remember that we have described
these regions of their inhabitancy as liable
(although fenced off against the highest
regular tides) to be inundated with those
great extraordinary tides which have always
happened from time to time in the northern
ocean. The Reader will advert to the
abundant multitude of people, which the
history of these countries brings in every
event of the war. He will recollect that
the great rivers and maritime coasts of the
west of Europe were well known to these
naval people; also the * portages over-
land which connected these routs with the
Rhone and the Mediterranean : he will
recollect the great fleets that they possessed
and commanded; and that even royal expeditions up the Rhine to the extreme of
Germany were not now for the first prac-
tised. Recollecting these things, and ad-
verting how they combine in this great
and astonishing event, as it appeared to the
Romans, when he reads that the Cimbri
and Teutones (according to a tradition

* Vide Strabo, Lib. 4. p. 189.

which

which L. Florus, lib. iii. c. 3. mentions,
and Strabo refers to), driven off their inhabitancy by a general inundation of thofe
low countries, advanced in fearch of new
fettlements * up the Rhine, by routs
perfectly known to them ; he will not be
furprized to find them all collected and
taking poft at the upper parts of that river,
fo far as it was navigable to them ; and in
the country at the heads of the waters of
the Loire and Garonne ; from the firft of
which, paffing over land by no great portage, they could fail upon the Rhone, and
defcend down that river; from the latter
of which, though by a longer and much
more difficult portage, they might arrive
at the Mediterranean, fo as to inveft the
Gallia Romana. To any one who confiders
the command of *marine* navigation which
they had to the weftern coafts of Europe,
and the common ufage in which they were
practifed in thefe voyages, all the difficulties which, not thus confidered, would
feem impracticable, will vanifh : and the
carriage of thofe fupplies, both ftores and
provifions, which enabled them to continue
fo long ftationed in thefe pofts, will be
found to be no more than that ordinary

* Cimbri et Teutones trancendêre Rhenum.
Velleius Paterc. Lib. ii. c. 8.

G   courfe

courfe of fupply which they fecured in
every expedition that they made ; and
out of reach of which they in no cafe
advanced. By making Aquitain, a country fettled in great part by colonies of
their own, the depôt of their magazines,
whence, up to their pofts, at the height
of the land, they would not only be
able to keep up their current fubfiftence, but to form advanced depôts, they
were enabled to advance on affured
ground. That divifion of them, which
afcended up the Garonne, kept up their
current fupply by their ravaging Celtic
Gaul and Spain, and faved their falted
and otherwife confectioned provifions.
In fact, all arrangements as to forage
and provifions, and the carriage of them,
muft have been and were regularly made,
and on an affured and permanent footing, as, amongft the other accidents and
events of the Cimbric war, hiftory
never once adverts to, or mentions, any
difficulties arifing from any defect in thefe
articles.

Plutarch *, in his Life of Marcius, exprefsly

---

* This method of raifing their fupply of forage and
grain from year to year, at the poft where they halted, or
which

prefsly mentions the nature of their march, as decided by their attention to this point. They did not undertake this expedition, as the effort of one campaign, by a hafty hazarded favage irruption; but they advanced year by year by different routs, and fo far only in each year as they could make good their pofts, and bring forward their concomitant depôts. They halted in the autumn, and there prepared their fupply for the next campaign; and fo advanced regularly. *Alios ad prælium hos ad bellum ire vides.*

When I ufed to read, in the Roman Hiftorians only, the accounts of this irruption, and of thefe people, as a fwarm of mere Barbarians, I was always amazed how fuch multitudes of people (200,000 at leaft), equal in number to a city of the fecond magnitude, which requires a circle of twenty miles radius, at leaft, of cultivated country to fupport it, could move and advance along a journey of fuch length, and yet every where find themfelves in the centre of fuch a circle of

which they took as ftationary, was, as we have feen before in the cafe of the Grecians, at the fiege of Troy, as mentioned by Thucydides; and as may be read, in Herodotus, of the Egyptian expedition.

fubfift-

subsistence. When I considered them as Barbarians, I could never conceive how they could arrange their line of march. In short, the whole which related to their existence, movement, and acting, appeared to me always inexplicable. But, when I had once learnt, from the accounts of their own historians, that these people were of a community which was greatly advanced in their experience of permanent supply, and in their mode of military civilization, (if I may so express myself,) were a nation of warriors, were a great naval power, had for many hundred years been exercised in foreign expeditions, understood perfectly the *res salsamentaria et frumentaria*, were all acquainted with the routs up the rivers Rhine, Loire, and Garonne, to the height of the land; when I recurred to the accounts of their incursions into Spain, and of their settlements (as this treatise has suggested) in Aquitain; their advance to, and their being able to remain so long on, the frontiers of the Roman Empire, ceased to be a matter of difficulty to my conception; I was no longer surprized when I read, that they repeatedly beat the Roman armies, until, finally, they were defeated by Marius.

Every

Every event and every circumftance arife now to my mind in the natural courfe of things. By the fyftem of their community, they were conftantly fending out fwarms and colonies ; and were always ready to follow them in national bodies. They were accuftomed to conduct the march, and the fupply, of a moving body. They had an experienced providence in that matter, both as to the collection, prefervation, and diftribution, of it. They lived under conftant habits of military police, and were every where, both at fea and land, a regular army of high-fpirited, determined, perfevering, warriors.

Having advanced thus far in refearch into the nature and hiftory of the progrefs of the maritime community, and of the naval imperium, of thefe people, if the antiquary will have the patience to go a few fteps farther beyond the period of this not lefs important than curious event, to events yet more decifive, he will find every thing that occurred, every event that arofe, came forward in the common and ordinary courfe of human affairs, long working to this point, the afcendency

which

which thefe maritime powers acquired over the great landed Empirè of Rome.

About the year 70 before Chrift, Freidle-vus Celer fucceeded to his father's throne, and purfued uniformly the fame naval fyftem. The Cimbri, Teutones, Marfi, and other inhabitants of the Low Countries, who were engaged in the enterprize above. referred to, were merely external parts, or rather provinces, of the Danifh Empire. The mere lofs of thefe people, to a nation abounding in population, was no great matter, however great their numbers. Freidleve purfued his excurfions into foreign parts, and was of fuch weight in the affairs of the great maritime intereft of the North, that Cæfar (as it is faid by the Danifh hiftorians), in order to keep the people of the Saxon fhores employed in attention to their own affairs, while he attacked Britain, made a league, or alliance, with him. The Danes and Saxons were in a continued and conftant ftate of rivalfhip, or war; and Cæfar allied himfelf with that party, who was not likely to interrupt him, againft thofe who were prepared and difpofed fo to do. While Cæfar was carrying his expeditions againft the inhabitants of the Armorican and Saxon fhores,

fhores, and againft Britain in the fouthern parts, Freidleve invaded the northern parts, and alfo poffeffed himfelf of Dublin.

About 40 years before Chrift, Frotho fucceeded his father. The fame fyftem being purfued, and the power of this empire increafing, he was engaged in a fucceffion of nine different wars; firft, againft the Sclavi; fecond, againft Gotheras, King of Norway; third, fourth, and fifth, againft the Huns; fixth, againft the Sueicos; feventh, againft the Norwegians; eighth, againft the Biarmlandians; and, laftly, againft Britain and Ireland. The force with which he invaded Sclavia, is thus defcribed by Saxo: *tanta autem navigiorum frequentia mare compleverat, ut nec receptui portus, nec caftris littora, nec commeatibus impenfæ fuppeterent.*

* The Hunns brought fuch great force of fhipping, and fuch multitudes of men, againft him, that, although he was able to raife a force to meet them, yet, he

* Saxo, Gramm. Lib. v. p. 84. Thefe Hunns are here fpoken of, as being on the rivers and coafts of the eaftern parts of the Baltic. This is the earlieft mention of them within the hiftoric horizon.

G 4.   found

found his finances unequal to the expence of supporting that force. The method he took to raise the supplies was, to send two of his principal vikingers on a joint expedition of piracy *, and to send out others to several regions, which were tributary to him, to collect contributions. *Et jam quæsiti latè sumptus, convectæque raptu impensæ, alendis abundè copiis suppeditabant.*

History continues the account of this naval imperium as the half of the royal dominion ; and, in the year of Christ 110, it was so considered by the monarch himself. " † Olave, in the last periods of his reign, as he saw his death approach-

---

* Ænevum regem et Glomerum piratarum precipuum ad Orcades perendorum commeatuum gratiâ dirigit, proprias cuique copias tribuens. Saxo Gramm. Lib. v. p. 89. The Orcades were at this time tributary, paying dane-gelt to the Danish kingdom, and were governed by a Regulus, or Viceroy. After Frotho had finished his wars, he appointed various Reguli over each district of the conquered countries, with condition of paying a certain tribute, certis tributi legibus oneravit. Amongst the rest, he appointed Revilus to govern the Orcades. These were Thegns, and the tribute they paid was Thegn, or Dane-gelt.

† Olaus cum supremis Fati viribus arctaretur. Frothoni & Haraldo filiis consulturus, alterum Terris, alteram aquis regiâ ditione præcsse : eam potestatis differentiam non diutirâ usurpatione, sed annuâ vicissitudine, fortiri jubet. Ita regnandi internecas conditione æquatâ, prior Frotho maritimarum rerum regimine potitus.

Saxo Gramm. Lib. vii. p. 120

3

ing,

ing, advifed his fons alfo thus to confider it, and to receive the kingdom between them under that divifion, not as two feparate *imperia*, but as two feparate commands under one and the fame united imperium : and, therefore, to govern and command in each by alternate annual rotation." That the maritime dominion was thought the firft in rank appears by this, that Frotho, the eldeft of his fons, took this command for the firft turn.

In the next reign, this double empire was put upon another footing. The elder brother, Haldan, held the command of both, as fupreme King; but, after he had prefided over the landed dominions three years, he committed thefe as a kind of inferior command, or office, to his brother Harald *, as regent ; and exercifed himfelf the marine department. I mention not thefe traits as marking the policy, but as giving proof, in fact, of the im-

* Perempto Frothone, cum Haldanus ternos circitèr annos patriæ prefuiffet, Haraldo fratri, regnandi jure perfunctoriè tradito, æiand'am : efque finitimas infulas quas à Suetiæ complexu finuofus aquarum anfractus divellir, paraticis populatur injuriis. Ibidem fubductis hyeme navigiis, de vallo cinctis, expeditioni triennium dedit. Poft Suetiæ manus injecit, ejus regem bello confumpfit.

Saxo Gramm. Lib. vii. p. 121.

portance,

portance, of the marine power and naval dominion in thefe northern parts at this period.

About the middle of the third century of the Chriftian æra, Harald Hylletand reigned; in whofe time the navy, both in its eftablifhment and difcipline, acquired very great advancement and increafe. He ftrengthened both his imperium and his arms by attaching to his fervices, the greateft adventurers of the times *. Aided by the fervices of Ubbo, a great Captain of Frefia, he fubdued the people bordering on the Rhine, and made them tributary. He recruited his army with the beft foldiers he could collect amongft them; and, confident in this

---

* Ubbonem, forore ei in matrimonium datâ, militem nactus, finitimos Rhino populos, tributo fubmifit: militemque ex ejus gentis fortiffimis legit. Quo fretus bello Sclaviam preffit, ejus duces [Phagen] Duc et Dal ob virtutem capi potiùs quam occidi curavit, quibus in commilitium receptis, Aquitaniam armis perdomuit. Moxque Brittaniam petens, Humbrorum Rege proftrato, promptiffimos quofque dividiæ juventutis adfcivit, quorum principuus Orm cognomento Brittanicus habebatur. Hac rerum famâ Athletas à variis orbis partibus accerfitus in mercenarium manum redegit. Quorum frequentiâ auctus adeo regnorum omnium motus numinis fui terrore cohibuit, ut eorum rectoribus mutuum conferendæ manûs aufum excuteret. Sed nec quifquam maris dominationem abfque ejus nutu ufurpare prefumpfit. Quippe quondam in Danorum republica dividuum terræ et pelagi imperium fuit. Id. Lib. vii. p. 139.

2   ftrength,

ftrength, attacked Sclavia, taking prifoners *Duc* and *Dàl*, the two famous
generals of thefe people. He attached
them to his fervice. Strengthened with
their affiftance, *he fubdued Aquitane.* After
that, turning his arms upon Britain, he
overcame the King of the Humbrians, and
enrolled in his forces every the moft
foldierly young man of the conquered
nation. He commanded the balance of
power in politics ; and held fuch an afcendant command in the dominion of the
fea, that no one prefumed to hold command therein but under his imperium.

There were, however, two marine
powers growing up in Norway and Sueïa ;
the firft governed by Sivard, Harald's
brother-in-law ; and the other by Ringo,
his nephew. Thefe were, perhaps, fubordinate, or inferior allies to Dania in
their beginnings ; but, driven into refift-
ance by the mixture of * jealoufy and infolence with which Harald held and exercifed his fovereignty over them, whilft they,

---

* This jealoufy was infufed into his mind by the wicked
arts of a confidential minifter, who wrought the brave old
King to a quarrel with his family, his friends, and beft
fervants. When he was worfted in battle, this minifter
knocked his brains out. Saxo, Gram. Lib. 6 and 7.

feeling

feeling their own power, ceafed to be difpofed to obey *, they revolted, and finally became afcendant and fuperior; and the Danifh empire, in its turn, became for fome time fubordinate.

Having now, in a kind of fketch, given fome idea of the rife and amplification of the naval power which *had laid its keel* in the North, and had been, by flow and regular progrefs in many ages back, extending itfelf; having brought down the account, which I have given, to that period when thefe people were ready and prepared to conteft the dominion of the fea, and of courfe the command of the maritime provinces of Europe, with the Empire of Rome itfelf; to the period when hiftory begins to bring them foward into that conteft; I will endeavour to mark to the Reader (in example) the firft

---

* In this war between Harald Hylletand and Ringo, the fleet of the latter confifted of 2500 fhips, though inferior in power. Suppofing thefe fhips to carry each 60 men, which is below the average, the army muft confift of 150,000 men. Harald's force muft be fuppofed greater. Harald's method of forming his fleet for action was inimitable, and peculiar to himfelf. But the fame wicked minifter, who betrayed him into this quarrel, communicated to Ringo this order of battle. The moment that Harald was told how Ringo formed his line of battle, he perceived that he was betrayed.

Saxo Gramm. Lib. 7.

fymptom

symptom of the importance of that power, in the scale of empire.

The Romans found it neceſſary, about this time, to eſtabliſh an office, and to create an officer, upon the precedent of the commiſſion given C. Cn. Pompey in the piratic war. They found it neceſſary, from the manner and degree of force with which this great Northern Naval Power preſſed upon their frontiers, to create the office of *Count of the Saxon Shores*, holding a command in chief over the ſea, and all the Weſtern maritime parts of Europe. Cerauſius [*] (a Briton, as Dr. Stukeley thinks) was appointed to this great command. This great officer not only exerted the power, which this command gave him, againſt the enemy, but ſo conducted the adminiſtration of it, by forming great and extenſive alliances, particularly with the Scots, Picts, and Saxons, that *he*

---

[*] This perſon was not the only Briton who, even in thoſe days and before them, held commands at ſea. Orm, cognomento Brittanicus, commanded in Harald's fleet in the great war between Dania and Suetia. Grim alſo was a great adventurer. The *bodes* and *bies*, or habitations, of theſe my Lincolnſhire countrymen, retain their names to this day in Ormſby and Grimſby. The two wapentakes, Loedbroec and Aſlac, retain alſo the names of two famous ſea-commanders, mentioned in the Runic inſcriptions, Lodbroeg and Aſlug: theſe might not have been originally Lincolnſhire men, but they had ſettlements there.

raiſed

raifed this department into a great political marine interest, which became of weight in the fcale of empire. Fixed on the broad bafis of an intereft of fuch extent and power, and fupported by the maritime revenues, this department became *a third power in the State* ; and Ceraufius arofe to the becoming a third colleague as Emperor with Diocletian and Maximian Emperors. At length, feeing that all was falfe and deceitful in the combined Imperium, taking this maritime into its combination as a part and partner, and that fuch joint empire would be ruinous to him; feeling, at the fame time, that his command was an Imperium which did not depend on the will of thefe Emperors, but ftood independent on its own bafis, he feparated from them, and eftablifhed this maritime empire as fovereign ; and, forming the fubordinate provincial legiflature of Britain into an independent one, under the name of a Senate, governed this empire, as an empire of itfelf, fixing the feat of government in Britain, with a fenate of its own.

If the Antiquary, who fhall ftudy the decadence of the Roman Weftern empire, will purfue, with attention, the beginnings and progreffion of this naval power arifing into dominion, and examine its operations,

operations, and the effect which thefe had in whatever hands it lay, by the little which the Author of this treatife (whofe line of life has not permitted a regular courfe of learned ftudy) is able to trace, he thinks much curious and interefting knowledge may be elicited as to naval dominion, in a period when it was fcarcely within the hiftoric horizon, except as it became felt at intervals by the irruptions which it made. When this is underftood as it deferves to be, it will be feen, that the people, who overran the dominions, and put an end to Roman Weftern Empire, were not Barbarians; nor their fyftem of attack the mere brutal force of Barbarifm. When caufes are confidered in their true eftimation, effects are feen as natural, and become underftood.

This treatife now returns to the Euxine and Mœotic 'Lake : it confiders thofe regions as the point from which, fynthetically, or to which analytically, the lines may be drawn, which mark the inhabitancy and the generations of the Teuts, as we have already done that of Cymri or Cimmerii. For, in the direction of thefe lines, fome *Gaëllic diverging branches* excepted, will be found all that

can

can be learnt of the inhabitancy or generations of thefe two fraternal nations.

* Both the Celts and Germans derived,
in their own account, their origin from
Düs, Dis, Tuis, Teut, Teutates, &c.
for, by all thefe names was the fame
Numen called. This fuppofed fource of
their race they called Got-Teus—or the
god Teus. Whence the Greeks, by their
mode of expreffion, made the name Cottus; as the Orientals framed therefrom
the tranflatitious name *Teu-Bâal.* The
word Thiôd (varioufly pronounced and
written, as Thiud, Dhyd, Dhiud, Tut,
Thiut) fignifies the general or univerfal
idea of a people, as applied to a community, or nation. Whether this word, expreffive of the collective gentile body,. became applied as a comprehenfive idea, like
Hobbs's Leviathan, to fome Numen, whofe
body was the people, and whofe foul was
their proper animation, whom the people
perfonified, and called their father, and
worfhipped as their God; or, whether

---

* Galli omnes fe a Dite patre prognatos prædicant.
Cæfar, Bell. Gall. Lib. vi. § 18.
Germani celebrant carminibus antiquis Tuiftonem deum,
terrâ editum, & filium Mannum, originem gentis, condi-
torefque. Tacit de Mor. Germ. § 2.

there

it was taken up as a general term to de-
note the body * of the people, *united into
a nation*, is of very little import. In the
firſt caſe it was a perſonal, in the ſecond a
gentile name.

A former part of this work, entitled, a
Treatiſe on the Study of Antiquities, has already ſuggeſted a line of inveſtigation, which
ſeems to diſcover that the Oiim, Ojim,
hords of the Tartar race, the Nomades
who inhabited the country lying between
the Euxine and Caſpian ſeas, and were the
original inhabitants of Tr'-oja †, ſpoke
the ſame language as the original inhabitants of Europe : and it gives an inſtance
or two from the ſcattered words of that
language of men, as it is called in contradiction to the language of the Gods, which
ſtill remain in Homer and Plato. That
they were of the race of Gyges, called by
the Orientals *Magog*, a fraternal branch
to thoſe of Cottus and Gomer, does alſo
appear.

* John Ihre's Sueio-gothic Gloſſarv.
   Thiód or Thiöt communitat pcpuli.

† Πολλαὶ ὑμώνυμαι Θράξὶ κ̀ Τρῶσιν.
                           Strabo, Lib. 13. p. 292.

H   This

This treatife hath already traced the proceffions of the generations and inhabitancy of the Cymri, the race of Gomer, from the earlieft periods to thofe later ones, when they firft came forward into the *Hiftoric Horizon.*

The Dteutfch or Thiotfch race remains next to be inveftigated. We have fpoken of them in general as connected with the Cymric and Gygic branches. Our inquiry will now purfue the lines of their proceffion, and generations in particular. From the name by which they defcribed themfelves, corrupted in its etymon and in its orthography, they were called by foreigners Tit-anes : from the name of their fuppofed firft progenitor *Got-teus*, the god Teus, they were by various deflexions of pronunciation called Gotti, Codhi, Gothi, Yutæ, Getæ, Chedoim, Chettim, and Κετεας ; and with the affix *ónes*, Teutones, Tutones, Gothones ; with that of *ingi*, Teutingi, Cottingi, and Tuthingi. They had alfo one common appellative given to them by the Greeks, in the name of * *Scythæ*, under which ap-

* Ἀπά τας μ᾿ν δὴ τὖς προσϐοῤῥιὖς, κοινῶς τῶν Ἑλλήνων συſγράφὖς Σκύϐα; ἡ Κιλτο-Σκύϐας ἐκάλὖν.

pellative

pellative arofe a fecond diftinctive appellation of * Celtæ, and Celto-Scythæ. The
common etymology of this word Scythæ,
as it derives from *Schuttan* to fhoot, and
Schutter a fhooter, as the people were
archers, I have taken for granted, and ac-
quiefced in as above. This word, however, being of Greek formation, may, by
the Greeks, have been referred in its etymology to this *appellative* Schutter, when
perhaps, as I believe is the fact, it was a
generical name, 'Sjutæ, 'Sgeütæ, *the remote*
Getæ or Jeutæ. Thofe remote Northern
tribes whom the Greeks called thus *Scy-*
thæ, called themfelves Σκολόται †, or
'Scoltæ, 'Skeltæ, from the prefix *Es* and
Kholtz, Gwold, Kald, or Kelt *Sylva*.

The word Celtæ, or Keltæ, as it was actually pronounced, appears plainly to be
a diftinctive appellative given or affumed,
as defcribing fome particular and diftinct

* Κέλται κατά τε σφᾶς ἀρχαῖον, κ} παρὰ τοῖς ἄλλοις ὠνομά-
ζοιτο. Paufanias, lib. i. cap. 3.
Si non Galatarum certè Celtarum vocabulo Græci Ro-
manique, Gallos, Germanos, Brittanos, Cimbros; gentef-
que omnes quæ τὰ ἔσχατα τῆς Εὐρωπης incolunt, complecti
funt. KUNIUS.

† Σύμπασι δ' εἶναι ὄνομα Σκολότας: Σκύθας δὲ Ἕλληνες ὠνομά-
σαν. Herod. lib. iv. c. 6.

tribes

tribes of thofe Scythæ, as Celto-*Scythæ*, Celt*iberii*, &c. The mode of explaining this matter will be fuggefted hereinafter. It will be fufficient here to obferve, that thefe Celtæ were originally called by them-felves Schol'tæ *, included within the re-gions of the Tribes, Achs, Thiots, and Getæ.

The reader is defired to take up here a reference to what I fhall fuggeft here-after about the nature of fome tribes, fuch as the Scythians and Celts retaining their fylvan life, whilft yet living in the forefts and uncleared lands amidft the fettled tribes.

The firft emigrations of this Dteutifch family, or nation, are found to have been made to the Weft, under the indefinite appellative *Achs*, a word in their original language fignifying *tribes*, rather than the nation in general: thefe Achs, as above explained, have been found under the more diftinctive appellative 'Sachs and 'Sacæ, a word compounded of the prefix *Ys* or *Es*, and *Ach*, fignifying the outer or *uttermoft achs*; which tribes, when they became *fettled* on the weftermoft borders of the continent, affumed, or had given

---

* According to the Greek pronunciation.

to them, the gentile name 'Sax-*ones*, or 'Sachs become dwellers.

To the South-weſt the migrations extended, by theſe tribes, up the Iſter on both ſides, and above the falls to the heads of it, where this river is called the Danoub. Theſe tribes were expanded on all the ſecondary rivers and waters of this great river ; and alſo to the Southward of it, in thoſe regions afterwards called Illyria and Dacia ; they made theſe their migrations under the appellative * *Daci,* which is literally *Die-achs, the tribes* : this became a gentile name written and pronounced Δαυοι by the Greeks, and Davi by the Latins.

The firſt range of the expanſions of this Dteutiſch family, or nation, to the South, appears to have been made under the appellative *Thiôd* or *Thiôt,* a Dteutiſch word (John Ihre's Sweio-gothic Gloſſary), ſynonymous to the Cymric word *Cumri,* ſignifying *communitas populi* : it is moſtly uſed as

---

* Δάκυς δ' τὰς εἰς τ'αναυλία πρὸς Γερμανίαν κ) τὰς τῷ Ιςρυ πηγὰς, ὺς οἶμαι Δάυυς καλῖιαθαῖ τὸ παλαιὸν ——— τῷ πολαμῷ ἄνω κ) πρὸς ταῖς πηγαῖς μίξη, μέχρι τῷ καταλακῖιν, Δανύβιον προσηγόξι- ν ν, ἃ μάλιςα διὰ τῶν Δάκων φίξεῖαι. Strabo, lib. vii. p. 304. Edit. Caſaub. 1620.

an

an affix, but alfo directly by itfelf. The expanding *Thiôd*, as it made its fettlements under this general appellative, acquired the Gentile name Thiôds, and Phthiôtæ ; and the country where they fettled was called Phthia, and Phthiôtis. They extended through all Theffaly, or * Thettaly, and Macedonia, Greece, Thebes, and Achaia †. The Phthiôtæ were Theffalians; and Strabo, lib. ix. ftates it from Homer, that the greateft part of Theffaly, or Thattalia, was Phthia. Phthia is exprefsly faid to be underftood formerly to be the fame as Greece and Achaia of latter times. ‡ Strabo fays

---

* It is worth marking in a note, that the name of the country Thattalia is, by an unconftrained and direct etymology, refolvable into Thuat, or *Tуat-dale*, an old Dteutifch word, for Northern vale.

Φθιαν τὴ, οἱ μὶν, τὴν ἀυτην ἐχι τη Ἑλλάδι ϗ Αχαϊα, p. 297. Homer makes Φθια in his time part of Ellas.

Οἴ τέ ἠχὸν Φθίην ἠδ᾽ Ἑλλαδα καλλιγύναικα. Ibid.

Εἴσι δὲ Αχαιοὶ φθιω᾽αι ἔθνος

Scvlacis Caryandenfis periplus——

Μέα δὲ Αχαιὴς Θατlαλία.

† Τοιαύτη δε σῦσα [fcillicet, Theffalia] εἰς τισσιεραμίεη διήρητο ἐκαλεῖτο δὲ τὸ μὶν Φθιῶτις, τὸ δ᾽ Εγιῶτις, τὸ δὲ Θατlαλλιῶτις; τὸ δὲ Πελασγιῶτις,

‡ Ὑπὸ τῷ Κροκίῳ Θηβαί εισιν Φθιῶτιδες. Αχαιοί δ᾽ ἐκαλῦνται ἱ Φθιⱳται παντες. Strabo, edit. Cafaub. 1585, lib. ix. p. 298, 300.

exprefsly,

exprefsly, that under Crocio the Thebans were Phthiôtides: and indeed all thofe afterwards called Achaians were, in former times, called Phthiôtides.

This *Thiôd*, or thefe *Phthiôtæ*, may be underftood as *expanfions of the community*, whilft the next range, who followed them under the appellative *Achs*, may be confidered as *migrations of difcriminate tribes*, and therefore called *Achs*. Thefe migrations covered the former and extended over Thracia, which is literally *Tre'-achs*, a diftrict of the Tribes; as *Achaia*, including all Greece to the Northward of the Ifthmos, is alfo the country of the *Achs*, that is, the Achaioi and Achivi.

* Hecatæus, the Milefian, fays exprefsly that even the Peloponeffus was inhabited by the Barbari, meaning * thefe people,

_____

* Ἑκαταῖος μὲν ὁ Μιλήσιος περὶ τῆς Πελοποννήσου φησιν ὅτι πρὸ τῶν Ἑλλήνων ᾤκησαν αὐτὴν Βάρβαροι· σχεδὸν δὲ τι καὶ ἡ συμπάσα Ελλας κατοικία Βαρβάρων ὑπῆρξε τὸ παλαιόν. Id. lib. vii. p. 222.

† I have not ventured to infert in the text an idea which I entertain, that the Hellenic, and other colonifts, called thofe original *old* inhabitants Graii and Graici. There was certainly a diftrict in Bœotia, or on its confines, called Γραῖα, which fome fuppofed to be the fame as Tenagra. Strabo, lib. ix. p. 404.

before

before the arrival of Hellenifts and other colonifts from Syria, Phœnicia, and Ægypt; indeed, the whole country, afterwards called Ellas, was the habitation of thefe people.

I will here venture to infert two or three inftances of Dteutifch words amongft the Achaians and Thracians, as a further confirmation of the opinion, which I have in my former treatife, as well as in this, in fome degree proved; that the primary old language of thefe people was *Dteutfch*: Λήιτον δε καλέϰσι τὸ Πϛυταναῖον οἱ Ἀχαιοί. Herod. lib. vii. c 197. This is the Dteutch word *Leet*, a court, ufed even to this day. Βϱία Θϱακιϛὶ πολις ἐϛι, that is Bury, fpoken fhort B'ry. as we commonly enounce Borough B'rough. Μη-σημ-Cϱία Μηγαϱέων ἀποίκος, πϱότεϱον Μενε-Cϱία, οἶϲς Μενα πόλις· τῶ κτίσαντος Μένε καλϗμένης—ὡς ͗χͅ ἡ τϗ Σήλυος πόλις Σηλυο-Cϱία· ἥ τὲ Ἀῖϗος Πϲλϲο-Cϱία ποτὲ ὠνομά́ζετο. Strabo, edit. Cafaub, 1585. lib. vii. p. 221.

Some of the tribes of thefe people continuing their fylvan, roving, paftoral, and hunters life, roving amongft the yet uncultured forefts, interfperfed, however, amidft

7

amidft thofe tribes which became fettlers, had various appellatives applied to
them, as Yaoul, or Gaoul, (Galli) and
*Αἴολες, which name is the fame word ;
for Æol, enounced with the Æolic
digamma Y or G, is † Yaoul, or Gaoul,
and fignifies migrators, or rovers. And
we learn that ‡the Doric and Æolic dialect
or enunciation were the fame. Thefe un-
fettled rovers were called by the *Hellenifts*
Πελασγοι §, becaufe they, like birds of
paffage, like the ftorks, for inftance, which
are called Πελαργοι, migrated from place

---

* Αἴολες τοπαλαὶ καλεόμενοι Πελάσγοι.
                                    Herodot. lib. vii. c. 95.
Οἱ δὲ Πελασγοι τῶν περὶ τὴν Ἑλλάδα δυναστευσάντων ἀρχαιοτατοι
λέγονται.   Strabo, edit. Cafaub. 1585, lib. vii. p. 226.
  Thefe ancient Pelafgic inhabitants were the founders of
the temple and oracle of Dodona. I have, in my former
Treatife, fuggefted that this Dodona is originally *Deu-*
dune, God's-hill ; and that the priefts, called Σελλοι, were
Seers, or Prophets: according to a word of the fame language, they were certainly called Βάρϐαροι, and are fo defcribed by Homer.

  † Exactly as we enounce with the digamma Y, and alfo
write *Eaork*, the old name of the city, York.

  ‡ Τὴν δὲ Διοσίςι τῇ Ἀιολίδι [γλώτῃ].   Strabo, lib. 8.

  § Οἱ τὴν Ατθίδα συγγράψαντες ἱςεράτι περὶ τὴν Πελασγῶν, ὡς κ̀
Ἀθήνησι γενομένων τῶν Πελασγῶν διὰ δὲ τὸ πλανήτας εἶναι κ̀
δίκην ὁρνέων ὑπιφοιτᾶν ἰς εὖ ἔτυχε τόπus Πελασγὰς ὑπὸ τῶν Ατθι-
κων κληθῆναι.   Strabo, lib. 5. p. 153 edit. Cafaub. 1585.

to place. Thefe Yaoul, Gaoul, Galls, or, as they are called Pelafgi, were every where in Theffaly, and even in Attica. Their appellative, when they fettled, became a Gentile name Αἰόλεδες, or Æolians.

These firſt expanfions thus operating, and thefe migrations thus taking place, were followed in all directions by more adult and independent tribes, who of courfe took more fpecifically Gentile appellatives, as from Cottus, or Gotteus, Cotti, Codhi, Gothi: from Teus, fimply, Teuts, Dteuts, Tuefchi, Dteufch, &c.; thefe were they who followed the 'Sacks in the Northern parallel directly Weſt. The latter of the above appellatives were, in thofe tribes who migrated Southward, converted into that of Getæ, efpecially by the Greeks; and into Chittim, by the Southern people who fettled on, or traded to, the coaſts of Greece.

Under this appellative * Κετεςς, or Getæ, they are found fuperfeding or fucceeding
ing

* Vide Suidas, verbum Κίτιυς. Although the Κετεο, whom Homer m.ntions (Odyff. lib. xiii. v. 520.), may be, as

ing the Daci *, on both fides of the Ifter,
up to the falls or cataracts. They are alfo
found fettling in the regions North of
this, away Weft, as far as that country,
afterward, and in later times, called Ger-
mania †, and up to the Hercynean foreft
and mountains : They, juft in the fame
manner as the ‡ Thracians did, as faft as

as in that particular paffage, Myfians bordering on Troïa;
yet Strabo clearly proves that Κεται, who were called Myfians were in Thrace, and called Ι hracians, definitively under
the general appellative Γιται. Οἱ Μύσοι Θράκες ο.Ἴς κỳ αυτοί,
κỳ ἕ; νὺν Μυσὰς καλῶσιν.
Strabo, edit. Cafaub. lib. 13. p. 204.

Herodotus, (lib. v. cap. 3.) confiders the Getæ a part of
the Thracian. And Strabo expreffly fays. Οἱ τοίνυμ Ἑλλη-
γες τὰς Γέτας Θράκας ὑπολάμβανον, ἄκεν ἐφ' ἱκάτερον τῦ "Ιςρε.
Strabo, edit. Cafaub. lib. 13. p. 204.

* Γέγονε δὶ κỳ ἄλλος τῆς χόρας μέρισμος συμμίνων ἐκ παλαιᾶ τὰς
μὶν γὰρ Δάκης; προταγορεύεσι τὰς δὶ Γέτας· Γίταςμεν τὰς πρὸς
τὸν πρὸς τὸν πόντον [fcil. Εὔξινον] κεκλιμένᾳς, πρὸς τὴν ἕω.
Ὁμογλῶτ οι δὲ εἰτὶν οἱ Γίται τοῖς Δάκοις. Ibid. p. 305.
Γίται ὁμωγλῶτλαι Θράξ. ἔθνη.   Herodot. lib. v. cap. 3.

† Τὸ δὶ νότιον μέρος τῆς Γερμανίας, τὸ πέρᾳν τη Ἀλβιος, τὸ μὲν
συνεχὲς ἀκμὴν ὑπᾶν Σεκβίων κατέχεται ἡδ' εὐθὺς ἡ τῶν Γίτων συ-
ῥάπ ει γη καταρκασμὶν εειη παρατεταμένη τῶ "Ιςρῳ κατα νοτιον-
μέρος, κατὰ δὲ τὰ ἄλλοι, τῇ παρορία τῳ Ερκυνᾶ ὀ ὑμνε. μέρος τί κỳ
αὐτη τῶν ὁρῶν κατιχεσα· εἶτα πλατινέται πρὸς τὰς ἀραίας μεχρὶ
Τυρίετας.   Strabo, ut fupra, lib. vii. p. 204.
See alfo Strabo, lib. ii. of the Getic Region.

‡ Ὀνόματα δὲ πολλὰ ἔχεσι καταχώρας ἕκαςοι.

they

they fettled, affumed, or had given to them, many Gentile names, according to the places where, or the circumftances under which, they fettled.

They are found migrating, under this appellative, South throughout all Thrace, Theffaly, and Macedonia. By the Helle-nifts they were called Κετεες Κετεες Μακε-τεες, and Μακεʃ-ονες, or Maced-ones; by the people of the South, Chittim, Cithoim, Ma-chittim, and Macedoim. Hiftory (Genefis, chap. x. v. 4.) fays exprefsly that the Chittim, or Cithim, were defcen-dants of Javan, that is, of Japetus, as above defcribed; " à quo," faith Hoffman, " Macedones orti," &c. And, continues he, the ancients ufed the word Μακετεες for Macedonici, as we find Μακετια for Macedonia. Now this word is a com-pound of Μα and Κετεες, fignifying the fame as Meffagetæ, the *hither Getæ*: that the Chittim were Thracian is cer-tain: and that the Κετεες, as Myfians, were in the earlieft times on the bor-ders of Macedonia, may be collected from Homer, as explained by Strabo: and the book of Macabees calls Alexander king of the Chittim. Thefe Getæ were

not

not confined to thefe regions, extenfive as they may be, as I have fhewn ; but Suedas (fee the word Κιτευς) fays, that king Latinus led the Chittim into Italy.

I have fhewn that thefe Jeutæ or Getæ migrated under this appellative to the Elb. We find that they not only paffed the Elb, and öccupied the whole country between the Elb and the Rhine, under the Gentile name Souêbii and Sueui ; but under the appellative Volc, Bolg, or Volgæ (by the Romans pronounced Belgæ), paffed over the lower parts of the Rhine, and drove off the Gauls.

Thefe people increafed in population and in the amplification of poffeffions and power, fo as to poffefs one third part of what was afterward called Gaul ; and in the courfe of time their population in-

† Μέγιςον τὸ γε τῶν Σͅηνων ἔθνος. διήκη γὰρ ἀπὸ τῦ 'Ρήνϐ μίχρι τῦ Αλϐιος. Strabo, lib vii. p. 290.

† ——— ad inferiorem partem fluminis Rheni. Id. ibid. § ii.

Belgas effe ortos à Germanis, Rhenumque antiquitus tranfductos propter loci fertilitatem ibi confediffe ; Gallofque, qui ea loca incolerent expulfiffe.

Cæfar de Bell. Gall. lib. ii. § 4.

creafed

creafed to fuch a fuperabundant furplus, that they fent off fwarms of Coloniſts to the Southern parts of Britain, who became fettled inhabitants of thoſe parts. Cæfar mentions this as taking place not more than fixty years before his attempt on Britain.

Thefe Jeuts, Getæ, &c. tribes of the Dteutfch family or nation, by whatever Gentile names in their feveral diftricts called, fixed their *marcs or marches,* and maintained an advanced frontier guard called Marcomannes, on the borders of Helvetia. Other tribes of them alfo kept up an advanced guard on the upper parts of the Rhine, which corps, by an appellative of their own language, they called *Guerjmannes,* which the Romans pronounced Germani.

The word German is a war appellative or military title, affumed as a Gentile name, not long before the Romans began to have knowledge of thefe people. When this *Corps de Guard* firft made their incurfions over the Rhine, they affumed, or had given to them, the appellative *Vics,* Victores ; latterly, faith Cæfar, they took
the

the name Germani. This military appellative is a Dteufch compound word, fignifying, in its firft fenfe, guardfmen. Waeringar *, from Waerja, or Guerya, a guard or defence, which is the radix of this, and compounded with Man and Mannes, is guardfmen, or guermen. The Bizantine writers, both Greek and Latin, corruptly and varioufly writing this word, called the guards Βαράγγοι, Varangi, Guarangi, and Varingi. This name is precifely, defcriptive of what thefe people were when they were firft called by it: they were a military corps, advanced as a frontier guard. When they firft paffed the upper parts of the Rhine, they were only an advanced guard of 15,000 men; the main body confifting of 120,000 men, foon paffed over after them; yet thefe were but as † an army *encamped* or cantoned, not as a nation fettled. Germani exercitiffimi in armis, qui inter annos 14 tecta non fubiffent. They fupported themfelves by the tribute and contributions which they impofed upon, and levied from,

---

* John Ihre's Sueio-Gothic Gloffary.

† Cæfar de Bell. Gall. lib. i. § 36.

the people, whom they held fubdued:
the perfon who commanded them was
known to the Romans only by his official
and not by his perfonal name. Arioviftus,
as pronounced and written by the Romans,
was *Here-oberft*, *Dominus Supremus*, the
Commander in Chief.

By degrees this war-name Germani,
from a general appellative, became as a
Gentile name given to them by foreigners.
The people within themfelves never varied,
when confidering themfelves nationally
from their Gentile name *Dieufch*.

A like advanced guard, but fixed as a
fettled eftablifhment, was kept a ftanding
corps on the * marc or marches next to
Helvetia. The corps was called *Marc-mannes*, and by the Romans *Marcomanni* †:
the corps was called thus as the ftanding
guard of the Marches or Frontiers; and
the commander *Maer-Bijuda* (from Maere
limes and Byjuden *imperare*). The Mar-
greeve, or, as we Englifh would call him,

---

* Fraeque [fcilicet, fedes Marcomanorum] Germaniae
velut Frons eft.

† Tacitus de Mor. Germ §. 42.

Lord of the Marches. The Romans, in their imperpect tranſlatitious enunciation and writing, called the corps *Marcomanni*, ſuppoſing them to be a diſtinct nation ; and the commander *Mariobudus*, taking this title of office to be a perſonal name. Exactly and in like manner they called the commander of the Teuts, or Teutones, Teuto-bodus.

They made the ſame miſtake in the appellative or title of office *Here-man*, the commander of the army of a province, whom they called *Ariminius*, as if it was his perſonal name.

Perhaps the grave Antiquary may think I carry this matter too far, when I conjecture that the Romans and Greeks made the ſame miſtake, when they gave to the leaders of the Celts and Gauls the name *Brennus*, ſpecifically as a perſonal name, while the word was only an appellative, *Baron*, the title of office : yet the following quotation from Joan. Loccenii Antiquitates Suio-Gothicæ juſtifies the conjecture, qui ſe præclaris facinoribus in bello præ-ſtitiſſet, nomen *Baronis* merebatur. And again, the word *Barum*, in the Norwegian laws, is tranſlated by the Daniſh word Here-man.

If it were the purpofe of this treatife to
purfue this line of refearch under the
pretence of hiftory, whilft it only means
to recommend and to fuggeft to the Antiquary an hypothetical theorem, I might
and could carry this farther. It is, however, enough to the purpofe of this treatife, which is to give grounds whereon to
inveftigate the fact, that all Europe in its
firft inhabitancy was peopled and occupied
by two fraternal branches of one family,
the Cumri and Dteutfch.

There remains, however, another defcription of tribes to be accounted for, I
mean the Celts, whom, as my opinion
perfuades me, I fhall fhew not to be a
different race of people from the Dteufch,
but tribes of the fame, perfevering as foreft-
hunters in their original fylvan life. Thefe
tribes ranging in the woods and uncleared
lands, as the Indians of America do at
this day, were, fo far as and wherefoever
thefe hunting grounds extended *, mixed

* Πρὸς μὲν τὴν Ἀδριατικὴν τὰ Ἰλλύρικα [ἰθ. η], πρὸς δὲ ἑτέραν
μέχρι Προποντίδος κ᾽ Ἑλλησπόντα τὰ Θρᾳκ.ά, κ᾽, εἰ τινὰ τέτοις
ἀναμεμίκασι, Σκύθικα κ᾽ Κελτικά.
    Strabo, Edit. Cafaub. 1585, Lib. VII. p. 216.

Ἔτι δὲ τὶς διαφορὰ κ᾽ παρὰ τέτας, τῶν ἈΓΡΟΙΚΩΝ κ᾽
ΜΕΣΑΓΡΟΙΚΩΝ κ᾽ ΠΟΛΙΤΙΚΩΝ.
    - Strabo, ibid. Lib. XIII, p. 407.

in the regions occupied by the Paſtor Nomade tribes, and poſſeſſed by thoſe who
became land-workers, who ſettled, coaleſced into communion, and were, in the
procefs of their progreſſive civilization,
organized and policied.

It appears to me, and I ſpeak from what
I have known in fact, that, in the firſt
ſtages of the progreſſion of human living
and inhabitancy on this earth, the human
race occupy it in its natural ſtate, and
therefore are homines ſylvicolæ, *Holtz-
boden* and *Woldſmen*, drawing their ſuſte-
nance in part from the wild produce of the
uncultured vegetation; and partly from
the produce of their hunting and fiſhing,
in animal food, which the rivers, lakes,
ſeas, and foreſts ſupply.

Quos rami atque aſper victa venatus alebat.
VIRGIL.

Of the Fiſher-tribes, and Sea-rovers, I
have ſpoken above.

In thoſe parts of the earth, where, be-
ſides the wild animals of the foreſt, the
feræ naturâ, there are found gregarious animals, who ſeem by nature to

I 2   ſeek

feek the foftering aid and protection of man : and, where man hath turned the exertions of his powers to the taming and rendering domiciliate thefe gregarious animals, the inhabitants of fuch countries become Paftor-tribes, and what were called Nomades. Thefe drawing the chief part of their fuftenance from the milk which their flocks and herds afforded, were of courfe attached, in families and hords of families, as fhepherds and herdfmen, to the fpot where their flocks and herds fed for the time ; and thus became, for the time, domiciliat fettlers: yet, as from the nature of grazing it would be neceffary (they who underftand grazing know this) to look out for and fecure the occupation of a fuccedaneous range of fuch fpots, in different feafons, in the woods and lands, as would afford brumage, pafture, and water, they muft alfo have and occupy fucceffive temporary fettlements, fo as to live themfelves under a * *ranging fyftem of inhabitancy*, changing thefe grazing, breeding, and feeding, ftations, according to the feafons, and the nature of the grounds fuited to them.

* Μεταγεοικοι.

During

During thefe temporary refidences, which they return to in their circuitous ranges, they naturally become *planters*, which work the women and children of the family perform by portions of labour in fragments of time. * They plant various kind of pulfe, which multiply the articles of food, carry the provifion beyond the partial fupply of the day, and thus create a certain feries of *permanent fupply* in aid of the fuftenance they derive from their flocks and herds.

Other tribes, in the advancing ftate of man, from the experience of this partial and temporary planting, began at length but by flow gradation of improvement, to fow farinacious and bread corn : this requires certain linked operations in working the land, and a continued permanency of refidence, from the nature of the culture and vegetation. Thefe tribes, therefore, by the procefs of their occupation, and the courfe of life it muft engage them in, became *Landworkers* and

* Σῖτον δὲ κỳ σπείρυσι, κỳ σιλέονλαικỳ κρῦμμα, κỳ σκόροδα, κỳ φύκυ:, κỳ κέγχυς.

Herod. Lib. IV. c. 17.

I 3   fettlers.

settlers. As the occasions as well as the increased causes of consumption, called for an increased supply, these landworkers would, as they actually have always done, begin to clear away the woods, and to deforest the environs of their habitancy, by making scattered and unconnected settlements as the local gave prospect of return for this heavy labour. This, and their driving the game from off their cultured land, would of course commit them in interferences with Forest-hunters, and, at the same time, expose them in a defenceless state to their inroads and depredations.

The *Pastors*, by the various intercommunions and intercourse which their occupation would occasion, would create and multiply the occasions, as well as give source to an advancing population. Their improvements in planting, as observed above, though not carried to land-working, properly so called, would prepare an assurance of sustenance to the prospects of an increasing progeny. So that these pastor-tribes would arrive at that situation in the progress of the human being, wherein an expanding population, with a mula multiplied increafe of their flocks and herds, would require more extenfive grazing lands in every ftation, and a more expanded circuitous range of fuch periodical ftations. Thefe tribes would alfo, in their way, encroach upon the forefts, difturb the hunt, and interfere effentially with the *Foreft-hunters.*

While thefe two defcriptions of tribes were advancing in their population, and, by the expanfion of their fettlements and grazing ranges, were ftraightening the hunts of the forefters, the population of thefe latter would firft become ftationary, and then decline. I mention this here as a confequence which would and did arife in the courfe of nature and time. But whilft they remained tribes of forefthunters, * thefe people,

Homines Sylvicolæ, belliq gerentes
Quèis nec mos, neq cultus erat; nec jungere tauros,
Aut componere opes nôrant; aut parcere prato:
Sed rami atque afper victu venatus alebat,
Genus indocile & difperfum montibus altis.
VIRGIL.

* A pueris nullo officio aut difciplina affuefacti, nihil contra voluntatem faciunt.
Cæfar de Bell. Gall. Lib. IV. c. 6.

I 4

unre-

unreftrained by any prefcribed modes
of artificial life, fuch as civil fociety requires, free and independent in thought
and deed; feeling for themfelves, and
acting of themfelves; living on the
earth in the ftate in which Nature
formed it; breathing that fpirit of fuperiority and dominion which fuch a ftate
of nature infpires in man *, would naturally defpife the land-workers as a *fallen*
degenerate race, drudges to their daily
and annual toil, and prifoners to their
fettlements—prifoners drawing their fubfiftence from flavifh labour and from the
fweat of toil inftead of the fpirit and man-
ly exertions of enterprife, and the glorious blood of arms. Thus defpifing them,
they would eftimate them and their property as much and equally their prey as
the game of the foreft; and they would,
in their free-booting excurfions, (juft as I
have explained above of the fea-rovers,) as
in the ordinary courfe of their hunt, make

* Ἀργὸν εἶναι κάλλιςον· Τῆς δὲ ἐργάτην ἀτίμοῖαϊον· τὸ ζῆν ἀπὸ
σολέμυ κỳ ληίςυος κάλλιςον. Herodot. Lib. V, c. 6.
Labrociniam nullam habent infamiam, quæ extra fines
cujufque civitatis fint. Cæfar de Bell. Gall. Lib. VI,
c. 23.
Id beatius arbitrantur quam ingemere agris, illaborare
domibus. Tacit. Mor. Germ. §. 46.

free with, and take fuch of, the produce
of their labour and property as they, from
neceffity, or even from the infolence of
caprice, chofe to have. I may add here,
as I faid of the fifhing tribes, they become prædatory free-booters, *not againft
but on principle,* fuch as it is.

In like manner, from a life of activity
and arms, feeling a confcious fuperiority
of enterprife above the quiet paftor, atten-
tentive only to his flocks and herds, and
confidering them as difturbing their hunts
and driving off their game, thefe hunters
would, as people of the like defcription
under the like circumftances ever did,
make reprizals by * *lifting* their cattle,
not merely when they wanted them, but
as a branch of the chace, within their
hunt, of more than ordinary fpirit and
enterprife. Thefe inroads, depredations,
and captures, thy would make, not under any idea of being enemies, or of com-
mitting hoftilities, unlefs oppofed, but
as a fuperior dominant race, doing juft

---

* I have here ufed a werd defcribing, I might fay almoft technically, the act of this prædatory capture, practifed formerly by the Highlanders of Scotland on the cattle of the Lowlanders.

what,

what, and no more than, they, in their ftate and circumftances of life, had a right to do, in the fame fpirit as their right of chace over the game of the foreft.

However, when, by the encroachment and interfering of the land-worker and paftor, as above defcribed, they confidered thefe tribes as doing an injury effentially obftructive to, and deftructive of, their chace and hunts, the foundation of their fyftem as foreft-hunters, and the means of their fupport, without which they could not fubfift; the cafe would be altered, and they and thofe other tribes would for ever after exift in a ftate of war.—Such war then would be fharpened into barbarous attacks, and in all the forms and circumftances of favage cruelty which a war of deftruction and annihilation, under uncivilized modes of life, is always attended with. For, fuch is the war of favages.

Yet, howfoever ruinous the hoftilities of thefe foreft-hunters may be to the paftors and their flocks and herds for a time; howfoever dreadful an enemy they may be to the thinly-fcattered defencelefs fettlements of the landed inhabitants; and howfoever

foever obſtructive and deſtructive to the operations of the land-workers ; yet, as theſe
Homines Sylvicolæ, as foreſt-hunters, could
not continue on any ground where their
game is diſturbed, and whence it is driven
off, and which ceaſes to be a chace or hunt-
ing-foreſt ; they muſt either change their
mode of life, and ceaſe to be a hunter-na-
tion, or retire to more remote foreſts and
hunts. Thoſe of theſe foreſt-hunters who
were ſo intermixed with, or ſurrounded
by, the paſtor and land-working tribes ;
and by their ſettlements and range of grazing, that they could not retire, would
decline in their population, as the room
for their mode of life was ſtraightened,
and as the means of their ſubſiſtence was
cut off: they muſt, in part, change their
courſe of life by degrees, and finally be
melted down into the general maſs of the
ſurrounding inhabitants. This, in fact,
was the fate of the Celts, intermixed with
the Scythians, Thracians, and other Grecian ſtates, with the Illyrians and Iberians. Thoſe weſtern and moſt advanced
tribes of migrating *Achs*, who continued their ſylvan life, would, as in fact
they did, retire ſtill more and more
weſt to the foreſts, as far as they could
find ſuch unoccupied. Thoſe on the Danoub,

noub, its waters, and its vale, would, as
they did, retire to the heads of the Danoub, where * Herodotus tells us they
were found to be, and thence to the Alps,
both Cifalpine and Tranfalpine, and the
Cevennas; and into thofe parts of Gaul,
where, as one third part of that people,
they were afterwards fettled as a nation become organized and policied.

The reader will, I hope, excufe me,
and permit me to infert an obfervation,
which I wifh him to make, that by this
account of thofe Celts, who fettled in the
fouth-eaft parts of Gaul, which I have
here given; by the account of the Pics,
Thanes, and other Cimbric colonifts fettling in Acquitain, which I have given
in the former part of this treatife; and
by the account I have given of the Belgæ,
migrators from the Suevi or Swuebi,
paffing the Rhine, and fettling upon,
and poffeffing the lower parts of Gaul,

---

* Ἀρξάμενος [fcil' Δανεβίος] οἱ ἰσχαίοι πρὸς ἠλία δυσμίων,
μῖλὰ Κινηίας, οἰκέωσι τὰν ἐν Εὐρώπη.

Herod. Lib. IV. c. 49.

Ἔςι ῥάχις ὀρεινὴ πρὸς ὀρθὰς τῇ Πυρήνη τὸ καλέμενον Κιμμι-
νὸν ὄρος· τελευτᾳ δὲ τῆτὸ εἰς μέσαιλαῖα τὰ τῶν Κελτῶν πιδία,
Τῶν δὲ Ἀλπίων ἃ ἐςιν ὄρη σφόδρα ὑψηλὰ, περιφέρη ποιέντων
γραμμὴν, τὸ μὲν κυρίον ἔσραπἶαι πρὸς τὰ λέχθενῖα τῶν Κελτῶν πιν
δία, κỳ τὸ Κιμμενὸν ὄρος.

Strabo, edit. Cafaub. Lib. II, p. 88.

bordering

bordering on that river; I have met the fact, which Cæsar states, of the division of Gaul into three parts, Celtia, Aquitania, and Belgia; and have moreover given some probable, I think an actual, account of the inhabitants of each part.

I shall presently consider the procefs of the changes which thefe Weftern Celts underwent. But I muft now firft advert to this *appellative* which they affumed, or had given to them; and, finally, to the *gentile name* they were called by.

Thefe Homines Sylvicolæ, as we find them called in a fragment of Nævius, dwelling thus apart, and in a totally different line of life and fituation from the paftor and land-working tribes, would of courfe affume or acquire a diftinctive appellative; they would naturally be defcribed, or defcribe and diftinguifh themfelves, as woodmen or woldfmen, by whatever word or words, as formed by different people, this idea may have been announced, or by themfelves. They were called by their *fettled* neighbours Gaoul, or Galli; and in their proceffion * Gallatæ;

---

* Gaul-aifæ—Γαλλάσαι Κίλτων ιισιν ἄποικοι.
Strabo, lib. 3.

by

by themfelves Celtæ, or Κελτοι, a title not only of diftinction, as to their mode of life, but of honour, felt, and affumed, as

Homines Sylvicolæ, belliqūe gerentes,

in a rank of being fuperior to the drudging land-workers, or the debafed attendant on brute animals.

This appellative, which would not at firft be peculiar to any particular nation of this defcription, or exclufively applied to any one people of this fort, was an appellative by which thefe woodmen and foreft-hunters * were called by every nation near to or intermixed with which they ftill remained. † There were Celtæ amongft the nations of the Scythians, the Indians, the Thracians, the Theffalians, and other Grecians, amongft the Illyrians

---

* Ὄψι δὲ κỳ τὰς αὐτὰς κάλεισθαι Γαλάτας ἐξινίκησε, Κέλτοι γὰρ καλα τι σφᾶς τὸ ἀρχαιον. Paufanias, Lib. I. c. 3.
Οἶμαι δὲ κỳ τὰς συμπάν]ας Γαλάτας ΚΕΛΤΟΥΣ ὑπὸ τῶ προσαγορευθῆναι διὰ τὴν ιυφανῆαν. Strabo, Lib. IV.

† Απογ]ὰς μὲν τὰς πρὸς βὅρέας, κοινῶς οἱ πάλαιοι τῶν Ἑλλήνων συγγραφεῖς Σκυθὰς, κỳ Κίλτο-σκυθὰς ἐκάλεν,
Strabo, Lib. II.

Τὰς δὲ Κέλτας ἀναμεμιγμύμενας τοῖς Θρᾳξὶ κỳ τοῖς Ἰλλυρίοις ἐξιπορθῆσι. Strabo, Lib. VII.

and

and Iberians. Thefe Sylvan hunter-tribes are diftinguifhed from the neighbour and furrounding tribes, not as of a different race, but folely as to their mode of life and habitancy; and were therefore called Celtæ or Κελτοι. This diftinctive appellative more particularly took place, as more particularly diftinguifhable, on the borders of the mercantile and land-working colonies of the Hellenifts, Phœnicians, and other fouthern adventurers, who fettled every where on the coafts of Europe from the Euxine fea to the Columns of Hercules. This appellative took place juft as the word and name Indian hath done in America, a name by which we Europeans, fettled on the coafts of America, call the Sylvan nations indifcriminately and univerfally from Hudfon's Bay to Cape Horn.

I defire it may not be here underftood as though I fuppofed the word *Indian*, or Anjou, to fignify a *Sylvan* man. It fignifies fimply the animal *man*, as diftinguifhed from the *brute* animal. However, when the Indian was afked, what or who are you? and anfwered *Anjou*, he took a diftinctive appellative to diftinguifh him from the brute animal : juft as the
Κελτοι

Κελ]οι affumed, or had given to them
their appellative Sylvans, as diftinctive
from the paftor and landworking tribes,
living on campaign and clear lands.

The antiquary muft here fee, that as
thefe Celts were expanfions of, or migrating tribes from, the original Dteufch
ftock, and that all, whom we have been
able to find, thofe who retired into Gaul
excepted, * had their inhabitancy, although
differing in mode, mixt in and amongft
the regions of the original fraternal branches; their language muft have been originally Dteufch. We muft fee that the
Celtic language was not, as is commonly
and vulgarly fuppofed, that of the Cymri,
either Erfh or Welfh. The Cymric, or
Cimbric, language, ufed and fpoken in
Gaul, was not the language fpoken by the
Celts, but by the inhabitants of Aquitane
only; who, as I have before explained,
were colonies and fettlements of the
Pics and Tha-genes. Neverthelefs, as the

* Φημι γὰρ καὶα τὴν τῶν ἀρχαίων Ἑλλήνων δόξαν, ὥσπερ τὰ
πρὸς βορρᾶν μέρη, τὰ γνώριμα ἐνὶ ὀνόμαι Σκύθας ἐκάλυν ἢ
Νομάδας, ὕστερον δὲ καὶ τῶν πρὸς ἑσπέραν γνωσθέντων, Κελ]οι καὶ
Ἰβηρὲς, ἢ συμμίκ]ως Κελίβηρες καὶ Κελκοκύθαι προσηγορεύοντο,
ὑφ᾽ ἑ, ὄνομα τῶν καθέκαςα ἐθνῶν τατ]ομένων διὰ τὴν ἀγνοίαν.
Strabo, edit. Cafaub. 1585. Lib. I. p. 22.

Cymric

Cymric and Dteufch language were originally of one root, being the language of
one original family. I can fuppofe the
Celts, more than any other tribes of the
Dteufch, to have retained many Cymric
words and expreffions; and that, perhaps,
they had not wholly loft thefe when they
became an organized and fettled nation in
Gaul. I can fuppofe thus for thefe two
reafons; firft, as they retained their *original*
fylvan mode of life, fo they had within
themfelves few alteration of circumftances,
which required new modes of expreffion;
fecondly, they having but little intercourfe,
or intercommunion, with the other tribes,
would have few occafions, and lefs inclination, to mix their language. The reader
will, perhaps, have obferved, that, in fpeaking of the various tribes fettled in Troïa,
Theffaly, Thrace, and Greece, I have
incidentiy mentioned feveral Cymric words
and expreffions.

But that the Celtic language, the language of the Κελ]οι, was neither fpoken,
written, or known, as any language fpecifically fo called in Britain, we have the
direct teftimony of the venerable * Bede.
                                      This

---

* Quinque gentium linguis unam eandemque fummæ
veritatis, veræ fublimitatis fcientiam fcrutatur et confit tur,

K   An-

This treatife has now brought my account of the *Celts* to thofe tribes who retired up the Danoub up to his heads; and took their range of hunts on the Alps, both Cifalpine and Tranfalpine; and, on the heads of the Rhine, and down that river; and in that third part of the country, afterwards called Gaul. They could not go farther Weft, as the weftern parts were occupied by the Aquitani, whom Herodotus, taking a part for the whole, properly calls Κυνῆ]αι. And they were repreffed from the lower parts by the Belgæ, as above mentioned.

In this fituation, ftraightened in their forefts and hunts, compreffed into approximation; increafing their planting branch of fupply; and in fome degree, and in their own peculiar mode, engaging in agriculture; they, in part, changed their fylvan life; and did, in part, coalefce into a certain *communion* of fociety. They of courfe, the three caufes of population herein confpiring, got into the progrefs of

Anglorum videlicet, Brittonum, Scottorum, Piſtorum, Latinorum.   Bede. Eccle. Hift. L. I. c. 1.
   Omnes nationes & provincias Brittaniæ, quæ in quatuor linguas (id eft, Brittenum, Piſlorum, 'Scottorum, & Anglorum) divifæ funt, in ditione accepit [Rex Ofwaldus.]   Bede, Eccle. Hift. lib. III. c. 6.

ad-

advancing population. The human-being, thus coming into approximation of the species, and into that inter-communion of the sexes, which society gives occasion and course to ; and applying the labour of the family to a rich and fertile soil, in a fine climate ; advancing to great surpluiages of provision ; would soon abound in populousness.

They became thus settlers, not fixed however, to private and exclusive property, but by a revolving occupancy of settlements, round a centre ; and no longer ex-centric. The œconomy of the family, and the labour done on the land, were chiefly done by the women, children, and slaves. The men still continued *forest-hunters* and *warriors*, not only as separate *free-booters* ; but from the conditions of their own circumstances, and from the nature of their neighbours, formed by degrees into organized bodies of confederation, under a degree of military subordination. In this very state were the *Celts* of Gaul (called by the Romans *Galli)* found when the Roman state first began to have wars with and knowledge of them. At the time in which these tribes first became a national community, and were organized into the

K 2   form

form of government, hiſtory may fairly, at leaſt the antiquary may fairly, ſuppoſe, (as there is no other period to be fixed on, nothing which contradicts it, and as it is the moſt natural,) that, at this period, the word CELT *firſt became a collective Gentile name*, not only as it retained the original honorary appellative of the foreſter, but as it was expreſſive of the character * of the warrior, a deſcription of themſelves which all man-kind, under different names, gloried to hold forth.

These people, thus become populous to a degree † of plethoriſm; powerful and military, partly from a ‡ temper of recoil, ſpringing back upon their oppreſſors; partly from a ſpirit of enterpriſe, natural to a people in their ſituation and habits of life; and partly from the § neceſſity of

---

* Gill, Gild, Kilt, Validus. Leibnitius, qui in Cel-ticis, p. 104; ex Pontano hoc adfert, putare videtur, Cel-tas ab hac voce nomen accepiſſe.

I. Thre', Suero-Gothic. Gloſſ.

† Abundans multitudo. Liv. lib. V. § 34.

‡ Fuit autem tempus cum Germanos Galli virtute ſu-perarant, et ultro bella inferent.

Cæſar de Bell. Gall. lib. VI. § 44.

§ Ac propter hominum multitudinem, agrique inopiam, trans Rhenum colonias mitterent. Id. Ibid.

Tit. Livius, lib. XXXVIII. c. 16. Pauſanias, lib. X. e. 19. Juſtinus, lib. IV. p. 6.

ſend-

fending out fwarms from their fuperabundant population ; made incurfions,
prædatory invafions, and, finally, fettlements amongft the Dteufch, to the Eaftward of the Rhine ; fent out colonies,
in very early times, before the Romans
knew any thing of them.

Thefe emigrating armies had the appellative Galli and * Gallatæ. The firft
word expreffive of migration, the fecond
of *migrating fwarms* from a hive.
Γαλάται τῦ Κελτίκῦ Γενῦς as Plutarch expreffes the word in his life of Camillus.

If the antiquary fhall, upon refearch,
find this opinion, which I have fuggefted,
to be true ; that the name Celt, however
it may be found, as a diftinctive appellation of tribes living the fylvan life, in
every part of Europe, in Illyria, Thrace,
and Greece, in the earlieft times of hiftory ;
yet never and no where exifted as a collective Gentile name, except in the regions
afterward called Gaul ; if he fhall alfo

---

* Validiores olim Gallorum res fuiffe fummus auctorum
D. Julius tradit : eoque credibile eft etiam Gallos in Ger-
maniam tranfgreffos.   Tacit. de Mor. Germ. § 28.

find it true that when thefe tribes fo become a nation, and fent out colonies; it
will reconcile and accord all the contra-
dictory * opinions into which the learned
have been led, and which they have each
maintained, concerning the people b:aring
this name.

If the Hiftory of Europe were traced in
its firft origin to the root, in fome fuch
lines as have been fuggefted, and in part
explained, by examples, it would be found
to have been originally inhabited by one
race of people traced up to Japetus or Ja-
phet; and that the proceffions of the generations and inhabitancy of this race

---

* 1. That all the nations of Europe were originally *Celts*,
that is, heminas fylvicolæ, foreft-hunters.
    Abraham Ortelius, Hardonen Hoffman. & Pellouiier.

2. That the Celts inhabited the greateft part of Europe,
Pezron, Vel er, Scaliger, de Bertz, de Cocceie, Spencer,
Mezerai, Gedoyn, & Le Gendre. Cluver, excepting how-
ever the inhabitants of Italy, is of this opinion.

3. Others do not give the appellative *Celt* to any nations
but thofe of Germany and Gaul.
    Volaterran. Glarean. Obrecht, Schelter, Leibnitz, and
    the Count de Bunan.

4 Others think the Germans alone were Celts, and that
the Gauls afterwards received the appellative as a name
from them. Browker. Marhoff.
    Vide Differtation of Mr. Schæpelin, § 3.

branched

branched in Europe in two fraternal lines, the Cymric and Teutfch, traced up to Gomer and Teus : as alfo, that the tribes of the Celts, part of the latter family, retaining the original fylvan life, dwelt amongft the Dteutfch, till, in procefs of time, they became a diftinct nation in Gaul; that all thefe originally fpoke one and the fame language; and that, however, from different modes of life, and government; from feparate inhabitancy; from innu - merable neceffities and occafions in the progrefs of the different lines of civilization of each people; feparate and diftinct, which muft create new, and borrow adventitious words, their language may afterward differ from each other; yet moft of the originally radical words of the Greek, Dteufch, Cymric, and Celtic language, will be found to have a near agnotion.

Thus much as to the point in queftion, who thefe people were. In the next refearch, what they were. This treatife wifhes to fuggeft, that that inquiry ought to be purfued by a line, wherein principles and facts combine. And it now proceeds to give fome faint fketch of that line.

Man

Man is by his animal fyftem, and by the paffions implanted in his nature, formed * *to increafe and multiply, and to replenifh the Earth.* The human race hath always actually increafed † in proportion to their approximation in Society ‡ ; to the fpace of land which they had wherein to locate themfelves and family § ; to the fubfiftence which the peculiar fyftem under which they live requires and affords. Whilft men continued living *the Sylvan life* ‖, gathering the fpontaneous vegetables and fruits of the woods, or as hunters catching the wild animals of the

---

* There are no bounds to the prolific na ure of plants and an mals, but what is made by their crowding and interfering with each other's fubfidence.
　　　　Dr. Franklin's Thoughts on Population.

† I have heard, when I was in the Indian country in North America, another collateral reafon affigned for the flow progrefs of population amongft them, taken from the following fact. That the woman fuck ing her child never admits her hufband to co-habit with her, until her child, getting its teeth, is weaned. This looks fo like to, and feems fo to derive from, natural circumftances, that one would be almoft induced to guefs from analogy, that the like muft have taken place in other nations under the like circumftances.

‡ Agreftia poma et recens fera.　Tacit. de Mor. Germ.

§ Dr. Franklyn's Thoughts on Population.

‖ Gen'que virûm truncis et duro robore nata
　— genus indocile ac difperfum.———Virgilius.

　　　　　　　　　　　　　　　foreft,

foreſt, for their food; they would, from
the mode of that life, and from the nature
of that occupation, multiply but ſlowly.
The hunter, removed by his long range of
hunt far from the women; abſtracted from
all feelings and ideas about them; abſent
long from mixt Society ; intent upon his
purſuits in the foreſt ; and in continued
training of ſtrong exerciſe ; does not even
feel thoſe animal incitements, nor thoſe
attractions of the heart, which in every
other ſituation are conſtantly ſoliciting the
man. The ſubſiſtence of the hunter is to
be ſought far and wide; his ſupply is *aſper
victu*; and he muſt always feel the bounds
of his lands ſtraightened. The Sylvan
Hunter Nation, from principle, never
could be prolific and populous, and in
fact never was.

A region, occupied and employed only
as a hunt, can give ſubſiſtence but to a
few ranging ſcattered hunters. I ſpeak
not only of what I may be ſuppoſed to
know, but what is of common notoriety.
" America is chiefly occupied by Indians,
" who ſubſiſt moſtly by hunting : but,
" as the hunter, of all men, requires the
" greateſt quantity of land, whence to
" draw his ſubſiſtence (the huſbandmen
" ſub-

" fubfifting on much lefs, and the garde-
" ner on ftill lefs, and the manufacturer
" the leaft of all), the Europeans found
" America as fully fettled as it could
" be *by hunters.*" The numbers of the
inhabitants, however, bore no proportion,
according to the ideas of the *landworker*,
to the fpace which they occupied.

The forefts and mountains of Europe
were, in the original inhabitancy, poffeffed and occupied in like manner by fcattered tribes of fylvan people, fubfifting on
the fpontaneous vegetation of earth and
trees; and on the flefh of the wild animals of the forefts. Such were originally
the *Celts* (by whatever various appellatives
called by their neighbours). It is common
to the Indians of America as well as to
the Celts of Europe, to have about their
temporary refidences temporary planting
grounds. Yet this temporary refidence,
this temporary planting and partial branch
of fupply, from legumes, pulfe, and roots,
have never led to agriculture, or the fixing
thefe fylvan rovers as fettled landworkers.
There is not, that I know of, any one
inftance of the Indians in America becoming either a paftor nomade or a land-
working fettler. And, I think, the courfe

4   of

of this treatife has fhewn, that the Celts of Gaul becoming fo was owing to other and external caufes.

When fabulous hiftory fuppofes the fylvan inhabitants of Europe * to have been compofed into fome civil forms, and to have received laws from Saturn, this was but the mere patriarchal government of authority, not of coercion, exactly the fame as that by which the Sachem and council-men govern the Indians of their tribe. Thefe people changed not their habits, or their habitancy, or the fyftem of their life. They approached not in clofer contact by fociety, nor increafed their fubfiftence to any fuperabundance ; they never, therefore, abounded in population.

Exactly as the American Indians have been fuperfeded in their habitancy, and driven off their hunts, by the European expanding his fettlements †, fo do thofe

---

* Compofuit legefque dedit.
　　　　　　　Virg. Ænid. lib. VIII. v. 322.

† Belli rabies, amorque, fucceffit habendi
　Tum manus Aufoniæ, & gentes venére Sicanæ
　Sæpius & nomen pofuit faturnia tellus
　Tum Reges, &c.　Virg. Æneid. Lib. VIII. v. 327.

fylvan

sylvan *Aborigines*, as they are called, seem to have been driven back by the foreign Eastern colonists and adventurers, who came and settled first on their coasts, and thence expanding, by their land-working powers, and the operation of organized government, their settlements up into the interior of the country. There is, however, this essential difference between the fate of the Indian of America and the Celt of Gaul; the one never has *yet*, in any one inftance, become a settler and land-worker, but has worn away in a languid decline to annihilation; the other, when there was no farther a field, to go in search of unoccupied forests, and undisturbed hunts, became a national fociety, became populous, took the forms and orders of organized government. These Celts became, although retaining the spirit and form of foresters, a powerful civilized people, who recoiled on those who had before pressed upon them. This, according to the principles of human nature, and the course of facts in the actual history of these people, hath been the fate of the sylvan hunter of Europe.

The progress of the proceffions and fate of the fisherman, navigator, and
marine-

marine-hunter, the fea-rover, has been
fketched above in a line wherein principles and facts feem to combine.

This treatife fhould now, in this place,
proceed to invefligate the origin and nature of thofe Tartar tribes and nations,
whom, in the periods of time which I
have been endeavouring to explain, I have
defcribed as not yet in *hiftoric exiftence*,
nor yet within the bounds of the *hiftoric
horizon*; who, as I have expreffed myfelf, were in a ftate of fœtation, preparing
to come forward in their due feafon; and
who actually, in the declining ftate of the
Roman Empire, did come forward, prin-
cipally as inftrumental caufes of the final
and total fubverfion of that empire; and,
with it, of the civilized world. This
treatife fhould here, in this place, defcribe
the origin; the progreffion of the generations and inhabitancy of thefe people; the
manner in which, with an abundant furplus of population, they advanced upon
the *hiftoric horizon*; the nature of the
incurfions and attack which they made on
the Roman frontiers, both as foreft-hunters, and fea-rovers, and afterwards as
organized armies. But the author having,

2   fince

since he prepared a draft on the subject of this part, seen the account of these Tartar tribes, and of their advance into the Roman territories, which Mr. Gibbon gives in his history, founded in so much more extensive learning, and illumined with so much better information than the author possesses, or pretends to, he, suppressing what he had written on this head, begs to refer to that learned gentleman's history of the decline of the Roman Empire. However, from an opinion which he hath many years ago formed, from what he imagines his own experience hath led to, of the *three races of man*, which inhabit this globe, the white, the red, and the black. He ventures to describe the nature and character of these Tartar tribes, which he supposes to be of *the Red Race*, distinct from the European White Race. The specific form of their sculls, the coarse texture of their hair, as well as their colour, mark them of a specifically distinct family from the European. Their original language, since called the 'Sclavonian, was quite different from either the Cumric or Dteusch. Although they fell into the same habits of life as the forest-hunters, the *Celts*, and as the Scythian Nomads, yet the temper of their mind was more ferocious, brutal, and less susceptible of human feeling. In

short,

fhort, they were not only in their body and in their mind different from the European ; but, if the human being has any ftandard, lefs conformed to that ftandard.

But this treatife will now proceed farther, as in the explanation fo to the application of this theorem, which gives the rule whereby to mark the fluctuating ftate of population amongft nations and people, according to their internal modes of life and their external ftate of habitancy.

The period of the greateft population of the paftor-nation, as a roving people of paffage, is that moment, when, having carried their grazing to the higheft improvement which their pafture-lands are capable of, and having extended the range of them to the utmoft extent which they can occupy, they draw a *fubfidiary part* of their fubfiftence from tillage and planting, without yet being fo engaged in the fyftem of the landworker as to become fettlers. This is the period in which they can bring the greateft number of men into the field; and in which they can emigrate with the greateft multitudes in a body.

Such are the fources, and fuch the principles, on which the population of the race

of

of men, in their various circumftances of inhabitancy, and life, depends, and from which it derives. Hence may be explained the reafon why the fame people, under different habits of life, and various circumftances of inhabitancy, may be at one time progreffive to populoufnefs, at another ftationary, and at another declining. This may account for that plethorifm of populoufnefs with which, at one time or another, almoft every nation hath abounded and overflown. Hence may be deduced a knowledge of thofe circumftances, in each people, which enabled them to fend out colonies, or even to emigrate in their whole body. This alfo accounts for thofe reciprocations of afcendant and declining power, which almoft every nation, in the firft ftages of the inhabitancy of Europe, hath felt within itfelf, and experienced from others. In the *vegetating ftate* (if I may fo exprefs myfelf) of civil community in thefe firft periods of inhabitancy, its capacities, its poffeffions, its occupations, are perpetually changing, as thefe reciprocally, and alternately, give expanfion to, or reprefs, each other. Hence the population of fuch community, under fuch circumftances, muft of courfe be in a continual fluctuation between increafe

and

and decreafe, or for fome temporary periods ftationary betwixt the two. One while it would advance to a plethorifm of populoufnefs which would exceed all belief in thofe who had not particularly confidered thefe matters. Such community, reported by hiftory in this progreffion only of its being, would appear as a nation having within itfelf an unceafing fource of population, which the common way of eftimating the nature of people, as they now are in a fettled and fixed ftate of fociety and government, could never account for*. Philofophers, therefore, with more ingenuity than foundation in reafon or fact, have fuppofed fome imaginary youth and vigour of the world; but all this is beyond the mark. Wherever, in any degree, any community hath in the prefent period of the world, exifted under like circumftances, the population of that community hath always advanced and increafed to a proportionate degree, of which the Britifh American colonies, and more efpecially

---

* To prove, therefore, or account for the greater populoufnefs of antiquity, by the imaginary youth and vigour of the world, will fcarce be admitted by any juft reafoner. Thefe general phyfical caufes ought entirely to be excluded from that queftion.

Hume's Effay on the populoufnefs of Ancient Nations.

L   the

the New Independent States, are, amongſt other inſtances, an example.

Although theſe nations, however popu-lous, cannot be * eſtimated in ſtrength equal to what their numbers render them capable of, until they ſhall have advanced in their civilization to ſome degree of union of power, and of ſubordination to lead : yet are they equally ſtrong as their neighbour nations of the like ſort. Hence, in theſe early periods of the inhabitancy of Europe, as this or that nation, in the Eaſt or in the Weſt, aroſe in its population above the level of its neighbours, like an aſcending wave it bore down upon thoſe below it. In this way one wave followed or met another, in perpetual undulations ; and the whole of the inhabitancy of Europe was like a troubled ocean, where all was in perpetual motion in all directions †,

---

* Θρήϊκων δ᾽ ἔθνος μεγιστόν ἐςι, μεlά γ᾽ Ἰνδὰς, πάνlων ἀνθρώπων· εἰ δὲ ὑπ᾽ ἑνὸς ἄρχοιlo, ἢ φρονέοιlο καlὰ τωὑτὸν, ἀμαχόν τ᾽ ἄν εἴη, κ᾽ πολλῷ κράτιςον τῶν πάνlων ἐθνέων, καlὰ γνώμην τὴν ἐμὴν, ἀλλὰ γὰρ τᾶτο ἄπορον σφῖ κ᾽ ἀμήχανον μήκοlε ἐ᾽γενήlαι.

Herod. Lib. v. c. 3.

† Μlαναςάσεις γὰρ δέδεικlαι τῶν πλησιοχώρων εἰς τὰς αἰσθανε-ςέροις ἐξαναςᾶlων.

Strabo. Lib. vii, p. 305.

as the temporary plethorifm of populoufnefs, in this or that nation, gave fpring
to fuch motion. It was not in any one
nation, or in any one period of the world's
fertility, in which, more at one time than
another, and more anciently than at prefent, the antiquary need look for the
caufes and fources of thefe plethorifms
of populoufnefs. Such have taken place
in all ages and in all people wherever, for
the time, thofe circumftances, which are
the fources of it, have combined and
operated. In the progrefs of the civilization of communities * every nation hath
found its population fluctuate from increafe
to decreafe, and at times become ftationary.
By thefe principles, combining with facts
like thefe, the antiquary will eafily account
for all thofe changes of inhabitancy, that

* Αὐξηθίνϵς δ᾽ ἂν ἐπίπλϵῖςον, οἵ τϵ Γέται οἵ τϵ Δάκοι, ὥςι κỳ
ϵἴκοσι μυριάδων ἐκπέμπϵιν, ςραϊϵιαν, νῦν ὅσον τὰς τέτϊαρας μυριάδας
συνϵςαλμένοι τυγχάνϵσι. Strabo, lib. vii. p. 305.

The like is reported of the Tectofages, Trocmi, and
Teliftobogii :—Εἰκὸς δ᾽ ἐκλϵλοιπέναι διὰ τὰς ἀθρόας ϵπαναςάσϵις,
ϰαθάπϵρ ϰỳ ἐπ᾽ ἄλλων συμβαίνϵι πλϵιόνων.
Strabo, lib. iv. p. 187.

Cimbri, parva nunc civitas, fed gloria ingens veteuif-
que famæ latè veftigia manent, utraque ripà caftra, ac
fpatia, quorum ambitu nunc quoque metearis molem ma-
nufque gentis, et tam magni exercitus fidem.
Tacit. de Mor. Germ. § 37.

fluc-

fluctuation of afcendant temporary powers perpetually rolling and recoiling * amongft the people of Europe, like the various and varied currents of a troubled ocean, running in all directions and undecided courfes. But he will find in the end, that when once the fpirit of melioration, and thofe principles which *humanize* (if I may ufe that expref-fion) the animal man, had extended itfelf from the borders of civilized nations, and began to operate amongft thofe tribes of favages, who ranged beyond the Tanaïs, *per folitudines finè fine diftantes*; then firft would the ftorm take a decided recoil, and, like a deluge, piled up with accu-mulated waves on the back of each other, and pouring down with accelerated force, burft forth on the borders of the civilized and cultured world. While this humanizing fpirit worked its courfe, in, upon, and amongft, thefe favage herds and clans (their population continually abounding to a degree of plethorifm) they would con-tinually advance in a contrary direction, and migrate in fwarms followed up with fucceffive fwarms; and force their way

---

* Quotidianis præliis contendunt quam aut fuis finibus alios prohibent, aut ipfi in aliorum finibus bellum gerent.
Cæfar de Bell. Gall. lib. I. § 1.

with

with a ferocious fpirit, and irrefragable
body of warriours, which more perfect
difcipline, with a lefs ferocious fpirit,
could not'refift.

Thus it was that the ALANS, increafing
in population*, *populofæ gentes et amplæ*,
advanced over the Tanaïs; thus it was that
the HUNNS, in numberlefs namelefs tribes
advancing on the back of each other, advanced upon the Alans ; thus it was that
thefe Alans, Hunns, and Tartar tribes,
united, advanced upon the half civilized
and half-fettled Goths, Sarmatæ, Jazyges,
&c. † Howfoever fuperior the Scythian
nations had proved to the Roman arms on
the extreme frontiers of the empire, they
were yet inferior to thefe Tartars in their
rear.

Thefe Nomade hunter-clans and paftor-
hords, who extended, as Ammianus Mar-
cellinus fays, lib. XXXI. eaftward as far as

* Καὶ πλήθει ἢ βίᾳ διαφέροντες.   Strabo, Lib. xi.
                           Ammian. Marcellinus, Lib. xxxi.

† Neque Hunnorum nomen Scythas, neque Romanos
Scytharum ferre. Eunapius.

the

the Ganges, and weftward (as * Saxo
Grammaticus finds) to the eaftern borders
of the Baltic Sea, were thofe people,
whom, becaufe they dwelt Beyond *the
hiftoric horizon*, the ancient poets and hiftorians defcribe as dwelling beyond the
borders of the earth, beyond chaos, and,
as it were, out of exiftence. At this
period, however, they came forward into
hiftoric exiftence, and became great and
principal actors on the hiftoric horizon of
thefe later times.

Of all thofe people above defcribed,
whether Cimbric, Celtic, Teutonic,
Gothic, Scythian, or Tartar nations, who
became finally the deftroyers of the Roman Empire, it may be faid generally,
that during their advancing operations
they never became fettled land-workers,
nor fuffered in any degree their inhabitancy to interfere with the principle of
their being an army. They held and
maintained *this principle unalterably*, which
they never fuffered any advance in the modes
of their fupply, or any improvements in

---

* Danicæ Hift. lib. V. where Frotho the Third is repre-
fented as engaged with them, both populous and powerful,
in various ferious wars, and fevere battles of enormous
carnage, about twenty or thirty years before the Chriftian
æra.

the

the ftate of their landed poffeffions, to break in upon. * Their cabins, huts, and tents, were mere temporary ftructures on the fpot, made of fuch materials as the local fupplied, or fuch as they carried with them. Thofe who were enabled to enjoy a more refined comfort of a home, had for their fleeping-houfes, covered carts and waggons, *a travelling home*. Although in this ftage they drew a very confiderable part of their fupply from tillage, yet the manner in which they conducted that operation never became a caufe of fixing them ; † on the contrary, they changed their feats, as from the habits of their life and habitancy they were always prepared to do, as new pafturage, perhaps alfo as

---

* Κοινὸν δ' ἐςὶν ἅπασι τοῖς ταύτη, τὸ περὶ τὰς μεΐαναςάσεις εὔμερες, διὰ τὴν λιΐότηΐα τῦ βίϗ, κ) διὰ τὸ μὴ γεωργεῖν, μηδὲ θησαυρίζειν, ἀλλ' ἐν καλυβίοις οἰκεῖν, ἐφήμερον ἔχϗσι παρασκευὴν· Τροφὴ δ' ἀπὸ τῶν θρεμμάτων ἡ πλείςη, καθάπϗ τοῖς νομάσιν ὥσΐ' ἐκείνϗς μιμϗμένοι, τὰ οἰκεῖα ταῖς ἁρμαμάξαις ἐπάξαντε·.

Strabo, Lib. vii, p. 294.

To the fame point fee Herodotus, Lib. iv. c. 46.

† Διὰ τϗτο δὲ τὰς μεΐαναςάσεις αὐτῶν ῥᾳδίως ὑπάρχειν συμβάνει, φερομένων ἀγελνδὸν κ) πανςρατιᾷ· μᾶλλον δ' ἐκ πανοικίων ἐξαιρϗνΐων, ὅταν ἐπ' ἄλλων ὑπεκβάλλονΐαι κρειτΐόνων.

Strabo, Lib. iv, p. 196.

Non fe urbibus tenent et ne ftatis quidem fedibus. Ut invitavere pabula, ut cedens et fequens hoftis exigit, ita res opefque fecum trahens femper caftra habitant.

new

new tillage lands (having worn out their old), required; or as they were driven off by more powerful hords and clans preffing upon them. It was not in thofe cafes only which arofe from neceffity that they were thus ready to quit their ground; but in cafes which arofe from the fpirit of enterprize; for, the fighting men of the nation, no ways tied down by the intermixture of their labor with the land, were always prepared, and at liberty, to march off. The Scythæ, when they made their irruptions into Media, marched off with their whole body *, leaving the women, having the care of the children, and the command of the flaves, to carry on the bufinefs of the grazing, of the herds and flocks; and of the houfe work. † Exactly in the fame manner, and under the fame habits and cuftom, their defcendants, la erly in the times of the Romans, called Germans, occupied their lands, cultured by the women, children, and infirm, while the men of the nation were never

* Herodotus, lib. IV. c. 2.

† Fortiffimus quifque ac bellicofiffimus nihil agens, delegatâ Domûs et penatinm et agrorum curâ feminis fenibufque, et infirmiffimo cuique ex familiâ.
Tacitus de Mor. Germ. c. 15.

attached

attached to the land, but trained in military exercifes only, were always prompt and ready to take the field. So that, although their lands were occupied both in tillage and grazing ; yet, of the people as a nation it might be juftly faid, Agriculturæ non ftudent.

This principle of not being mixt with the fyftem of landworking, or attached to the land, continued invariably to be obferved in every progreffion and gradation of improvement in their habitancy, fo far as refpected the men of the nation. Even where, and at the time when, the community occupied the lands, as a landed and landworking people, it was in fuch manner as never intrenched upon this principle. The lands were the property of the community : the individuals had no fixt exclufive private property in them. There appear to have been two methods of arranging this fyftem of œconomy and police. One was to divide the community into watches and wards. The bufinefs of the watch of the year was in its turn to take the field, as the army of the nation. The reft of the community carried on the care and conduct of the fupply. The next year the foldier became

again

again a land-worker; and another watch
was taken out of the body of land-workers *.
This mode of occupancy and culture, and
this reciprocation of labour and military
fervice, enabled the nation by habit, as in
the ordinary courfe and fyftem of its life,
to act as a military corps, living in camp,
acting either defenfively or offenfively without being ftopt through a want in the fupply, or being obftructed by difficulties in it ;
for, this was all the while going on unin-
terrupted and undifturbed. The men of the
nation had no private property, no home,
nor even a dwelling, for longer than a
year. The taking, therefore, the field
for war; or the removing their feats in
meafures of migration, was only changing
their annual fields *in a right line that advanced*, inftead of doing the fame thing, as
of courfe, in a circulating one which re-
volved into itfelf.

The other method was, as follows, deriving from the fame principle, and guard-

---

* Cæfar de Bell. Gall. lib. IV. § 1, exprefsly defcribes
this method as a cuftom of the Suevi. Ii centum Pagos
habere dicuntur, ex quibus, quotannis finguli millia arma-
torum, bellandi caufâ fuis ex finibus educunt. Reliqui
domi manent, *pro fe atque illis colunt.* Hi rurfus invicem
anno poft in armis, funt illi domi remanent. Sic neque
agricultura, neque ratio, neque ufus belli intermittitur:
fed privati ac feparati agri apud eos nihil eft, neque lon-
gius anno remanere uno in loco, incolendi caufa licet.

ing

ing the same fyftem. The lands were
the property of the ftate; there was no
private property: no individual was al-
lowed to be a fixt fettler, or to have a
private home. The magiftrates granted
out the lands annually to fucceffive pof-
feffors *per vices* *. They apportioned thofe
to each family or clan, according to the
numbers in each. Each family or clan
divided thefe again amongft themfelves,
to fuit their own convenience. It feems

---

* Agri pro numero cultorum ab univerfis, per vices, oc-
cupantur, quos mox inter fe fecundum dignationem par-
tiuntur. Facilitatem partiendi camporum fpatia præftant.
Arva per annos mutant, et fupereft ager nec enim ubertate
et amplitudine foli labore contendunt ut pomoria conferant,
et prata fepiant et hortos rigent. Sola terræ feges impera-
tur. Tacitus de Mor. Germ. § 96.

Nec quifquam ægri modum certum, aut fines proprios
habet; fed magiftratus ac principes in annos fingulos, gentibus cognationibufque hominum, qui unà coierunt, quantum iis, et quo loco vifum eft, attribuunt agri, atque anno
pos alio tranfire cogunt. Ejus rei multas afferunt caufas;
ne affiduâ confuetudine capti ftudium belli gerendi agricul-
turâ commutent; ne latos fines parare ftudeant: potentio-
refque humiliores poffeffionibus expellant; ne accuratius,
ad frigora et æftus vitandos, ædificent; ne qua oriatur
pecuniæ cupiditas, &c.
Cæfar de Bell. Gall. lib. IV. § 22.

Servis, non in noftrum modum defcriptis per familiam
minifteriis, utuntur. Frumenti modum Dominus, aut
pecoris, aut veftis, ut colono injungit: et Servus hac-
tenùs paret. Cætera domûs officia uxor et liberi exfequun-
tur. Tacit. de Mor. Germ. § 25.

to

to me that the *arva*, or that part of .the lands which were appropriated for planting and tillage, were thofe which were changed annually whilft the *agri*, and other lands, remained in common. The people themfelves, who obferved this cuftom, give, amongft others, this very politic reafon for their obfervance of it. 1ft. To guard againft the rife in the human breaft of that idea, fo natural to it, the *love of home*, which, attaching itfelf to the habits of domeftic life, would foon lofe the fpirit of the military. 2dly, To prevent thofe inequalities in power and intereft amongft men, which always arife out of inequalities of property, to the difturbance of the peace, and the corruption of the liberty and virtue of the community.

Even in thofe cafes wherein it fhould almoft feem as if one of the principals of the nations had private exclufive landed property (although I cannot but think, that the property here fpoken of was the ufual allotment made in the ufual way), thefe principal people were never the more *land-workers*, or fettlers; they leafed out their lands to fervant-hufbandmen, on condition of a rent in kind, a certain

I   portion

portion of corn, cattle, and cloathing; and, as to the home or *cots-work*, that was done by the women and children of the family.

The men of the nation lived totally exempt from all labour. * If they were not engaged in hunting, in any military excursions, or in actual war, they gave themselves up to drinking, sleeping, or play. This vicious idleness was not, unless perhaps in the impracticable parts of winter, the general turn of the people. † In general their whole life was employed either in hunting, or in some of those expeditions which became a regular military training. They formed military companies under young men whose character and expectations not only gave them command, but made them, as it were, the seat and center of the spirit and honor of the company. Under establishments formed by this spirit of subordination and discipline, the young men of the nation (if their own

---

* Quoties bella non ineunt, non multum venatibus, plus per otium transigunt, dediti somno, ciboque.
　　　　　　　　　　　　Tacit. de Mor. Germ. § 15.

† Vita omnis in venationibus atque in studiis rei militaris confistit.　　　Cæsar de Bell. Gall. lib. VI. § 21.

nation

nation was at peace) either engaged as vo-
lunteers in the wars of their neighbours;
or * undertook as freebooters (juft as we
have feen above in the naval pirates) prædatory excurfions. or colonizing migrations, which generally, in the courfe of
human events, prepared the way to national invafions and actual conquefts. + This
fyftem of warfare, from the nature of their
inhabitancy, from the fpirit of this character, became, as it were, the ordinary
courfe of their life. The antiquary will
have feen, that with thofe nations, who
ftill continued hunters, thefe expeditions
required little more preparation of fupply
than their ordinary hunting parties: That
the game and the wild fruits of the woods,
the fifh of the waters, together with fuch
dried millet and fuch other grain as was
drawn from their planting grounds, became
a certain fupply: That thofe who had made
farther advances in fociety, and farther improvements in the modes of living, had not

* Latrocinia nullam habent infamiam, quæ extra fines
cujufque civitatis fiunt.
Cæfar de Bell. Gall. lib. VI. § 21.

+ Ex latrociniis occultis et raris, a lenta impunitate
adolefcentem in pejus audaciam, ad bella gravia proru-
perunt. Amm. Marcell. lib. XIV. § 2.

only

only arrived at the means of abundance in their fupply, but had applied the care and art of giving continuance and permanency to it. The paftor-hords were fuch perfect graziers, and fo well knew the ftate of the feed of the country, that they could * *combine their marches with the range of pafture*, fo as to be able to drive their herds and flocks, or at leaft fuch part thereof as was neceffary, along with them. From the milk and flefh of thefe they had an attendant courfe of fupply. They had a method of kiln-drying their corn and grain. They had the art of conferving (and may I not fay alfo † flefh ?) by falting. They made various confections from milk, *lac concretum*, curds, cheefe, and butter. Thofe who had advanced ftill farther, fo as to draw part of their fub-fiftance from tillage, underftood the

---

* They could not drive thefe in any direction which they pleafed, they muft be determined by the ftate of the feed, *ut invitavere pabula*. Their march therefore muft be *a combination of the line of march with the range of pafture*.

† This, particularly lard and bacon, &c. had been long an article of commerce drawn from Belgia, for the fupply of the Roman market; as alfo from the Sequani ; alfo from Spain, both without as well as within the Streights ; alfo from Pontus, which was the prime market for the *Taracheia*.
See Strabo, lib. IV. p. 97, 144, 197.

method

method of grinding their corn, and of preferving * it in *flour* for months. The antiquary will here find, that they had all the articles of permanent ftores for a campaign.

The antiquary that examines next the means of the carriage of thefe ftores and provifions will find, that, befides what each man carried himfelf, this bufinefs of the *res portatoria* was little more than what they had in conftant ufe for their annual changes of their habitations, or the occafional changes of their feeding grounds : they rather exceeded, even to embarraf-ment, in the number of their † *carrs* and *impedimenta*, without which they never moved.

It is a curious fact, well worth remark-ing, that whilft we read of the difficulties and deficiencies which the Romans, even Cæfar himfelf, found in the *re frumentariâ*

---

* Trium menfium molita cibaria fibi quemque domo afferre jubent.   Cæfar de Bell. Gall. lib. I. § 4.

† Magna enim mulⁱtudo carrorum etiam expeditos. fequi Gallos confuevit. Cæfar de Bell. Gall. lib. VIII. § 14.
     Equites ex Gallia cum multis carris magnifque impedi-mentis, ut fert Gallica confuetudo.   Lib. I. § 51.

et

et portatoriá, fuch as at times obftructed his progrefs ; there are not, that I recollect, the like inftances of the like difficulties to be found, in the movements and marches of thefe Barbarians, as they are called, even in a long line of march quite acrofs the continent. They underftood this bufinefs of *fupplying a moving body* ; and practifed it as in the ordinary courfe of their œconomy and police.

When the antiquary fhall have confidered, as above, the populoufnefs of thefe nations, in the periods of their plethoriſm ; fhall have confidered from the nature and conftitution of their community, in thofe periods of the progreffion of their civilization, the proportion of numbers, beyond what any other community in any other ftage of civilization could, they could and did bring into the field, as their ordinary army, generally about one fourth, befides what, on the emergency of occafions, they could ftill bring forward ; he will fee that they muft outnumber, in the line and point of action, empires much more numerous in people than themfelves. In the vegetating ftate (if I may fo exprefs myfelf) of civil community, its capacities, its occupations, its inhabitancy, and

M   oc-

occupancy, are perpetually changing, as thefe reciprocally give expanfion to or reprefs each other. The population of fuch a community will be, under fuch circumftances, in a continual fluctuation between increafe and decreafe, or perhaps for fome periods ftationary between the two. One while it will advance to a *plethorifm*, which would exceed the belief of thofe who have not confidered the matter in this light. Such community would appear, if reported in hiftory, in this period only of its being, as an unceafing fource of population, which the common way of eftimating nations would not account for. And yet, perhaps, the ftate of the fame nation, reported in fome other periods of its exiftence, would feem directly to contradict all this.

When the antiquary fhall have thus confidered their population and populoufnefs, the ftate of their fupply, *their mobility as an armed body*, he will inquire into the ftrength, activity, and fpirit of difcipline, by which they operated ; he will have feen above, that as every individual was a warrior, fo the whole community was an army; and their country a fyftem of camps; having its advanced

3 · guards,

guards, its warjamannes, and marcomannes, its watches and wards, and all·
its rotine of duty; he will fee this body
not only naturally, but artificially and
fcientifically, organized into *active ftrength.*
When farther he confiders * the fpirit of
military order and attraction to a center,
in which the individual war-companies
were trained, and with which they were
animated; and then extends his view to
fee how this gave life to the very foul
of the whole nation; he will view thefe
people advancing in a very different character from that of *Barbarians;* he will
fee them in *number, power, activity, fpirit,*
and *conduct,* equal to the enterprizes which
they undertook, and to the fuccefs with
which they executed them, in their incurfions into, and invafions of, the Roman
domains; and that the impreffions, which

---

* Infignis nobilitas, aut magna patrum merita, principis
dignationem etiam adolefcentibus affignant. Cæteris 'ro-
buftioribus ac jampridem probatis aggregantur. Nec ru-
bor inter comites afpici. Gradus quinetiam et ipfe comi-
tatus habet, judicio ejus quem fectantur. Magnaque et
comitum æmulatio, quibus primus apud principem fuum
locus; et principum cui plurimi et acerrimi comites. Cum
ventum in aciem, turpe principi virtute vinci; turpe co-
mitatui virtutem principis non adæquare. Jam vero in-
fame in omnem vitam, ac probrofum, fuperftitem principi
fuo, ex acie receffiffe, &c. &c.
Tacitus de Mor. Germ. § 13, 14.

they

they made, were not the mere explosions of brutal force; but that, on the contrary, they were *effects derived, in the ordinary course of human events, from reasoning and design, conducted with spirit and art* *.

When the antiquary comes to examine those more serious attacks; which afterward actually penetrated and over-ran, and finally overturned, from its very base, the Roman empire; he will have occasion to observe how these reiterated incursions, and a perpetual warfare, trained these people to an actual use, and habit of arms, *as an army*; and how also the very repulses they met with, and the repression, by which for a time they were forced back, served only to compress them into a closer texture, and wrought them, by degrees, into a steely temper of recoil, which the Roman arms could not repel: he will have occasion to examine (as we have already done in part, respecting the people of the Baltic

---

* Multum (ut inter Germanos) rationis ac solertiæ; præponere electos, audire præpositos, nosse ordines, intelligere occasiones, differre impetus, disponere diem, vallare noctem, fortunam inter dubia, virtutem inter certa, numerare: quodque rarissimum est, nisi ratione disciplinæ concessum, plus reponere in duce quam in exercitu.

Tacitus de Mor. Germ. § 30.

and

and Saxon coasts, on the Rhine and the
rivers of Gaul,) the rise of a naval power
on the Euxine, the Danube, and the
rivers communicating with it ; which became interwoven with the landed power;
which facilitated all the communications
of its union and communion ; which
gave more free and extensive powers of
movement to it ; and, like the veins of
the human body, gave circulation, permanency, and certainty of supply, to any
extent of numbers which were brought
into the field : he will find that as the
Cimbri, Teutones, Saxones, Goths, and
Vandales, advanced up the Rhine, and
up the rivers of Gaul, to the gates * of
Italy, on the West sides ; so the Jazyges,
Goths, Scythæ, Sarmatæ, Hunns, and
Alans, advanced up the Danube, the
Save, and Drave, to the gates also of
Italy, on the Eastern side. † Strabo de-
scribes the *portages* from these waters to
those which run into the two seas, the
superior and inferior ; ‡ the one rout by

* Cláuſtra Italiæ—Lucius Florus—

† Strabon. Geog. lib. VII. p. 314; alſo lib. IV. p. 189.

‡ This rout may fairly be ſuppoſed to be known in thoſe
early times of navigation to which the fable of the Argonautic expedition is referred. See Diodorus Siculus, lib. IV.

Aquileia

Aquileia and Tergefta, now Trieft; the other by the Arar and Rhodanus. Thefe were the common mercantile routs, and were as well known to the people of Gaul and Germany, as to the Romans; and were ufed by both for the conveyance of their provifions and military ftores, as the one or the other held the command at the time.

This treatife has already drawn a fketch of that naval power which commanded the Baltic, and the North Sea or Saxon fhores, the Britifh ifles, the Weftern coafts, as alfo the navigation of the Rhine and of the rivers of Gaul.

There remain in hiftory but very few traces, and thofe quite detached. of the map of navigation on the Eaft of Europe; and all the moft early accounts are fo deformed with fable, that it is fcarcely pof-fible to form any idea of them. It is how-ever. certain, that the fea, afterwards called by the Hellenifts the Euxine, was navi-gated by fifhermen, traders, and pirates*, in the earlieft time, as alfo by bold and daring adventurers, who braved the pirates,

* Strabo, lib. XI. p. 495.

from

from whofe cruelties it was originally called
the Inhofpitable Sea. The Phœnicians or
Ægyptians pufhed their commercial enterprizes into this fea, and fettled colonies on its Eaftern coafts. The Hellenic
Trojans, and afterwards the Greeks, poffeffed the navigation and dominion of this
fea; and made many trading fettlements;
and eftablifhed many colonies, in its Weftern borders. In fhort, this Euxine fea
was, in ancient times, one of the principal marts of the then commercial world;
all the rivers which ran into it were navigated, and the length of them were
reckoned by days navigation. The Ifter,
called in its upper part the Danube *, had
fixty rivers, which ran into it, all navigable †. The very firft account which hiftory gives of thefe naval inhabitants of the
Euxine, as connected with Rome. is in
Trajan's time, when, ‡ profiting of the
alliance of the naval people, who dwelt
on the coafts of the Euxine, he efta-

---

* Amnis Danubius, fexaginta navigabiles pænè recipiens
fluvios, feptem oftiis erumpit in Mare.
　　　　　　　　　　　Amm. Marcell. lib. XXII. § 8.

† Herod. lib. IV. chap. 53.

‡ Eutropius, lib. VIII. c. 2.

M 4　　　　　　blifhed

bliſhed the command of the Danube, extended to its mouth. But we find that
when the Goths and other Northern
people beyond the Danube, by alliance or
otherwiſe had the aſſiſtance of this ſame
naval power, they were able to make ef-
fectual incurſions, not only upon the remote provinces, but upon the very limits
of the empire itſelf up the Danube.

Zoſimus ſays, that they penetrated
through every part of Illyria, and even
into Italy. By the aſſiſtance of this naval
power they firſt invaded Aſia in the years
258 and 259, of the Chriſtian æra, and
a ſecond time by a like naval expedition
in 266 ; and in the year 267 ſailed up
the Danube into the heart of the Roman
dominions, *multa gravia in ſolo Romano
fecerunt.* At the ſame time the Heruli,
with 500 ſhips, forced their courſe
through the Boſphorus, and ravaged both
the Aſiatic and Greek coaſts of the Ægean.
This expedition of the Goths, &c. up
the Danube, was in the time of Claudius * ; and it is from the letters which

* Trecenta viginta millia barbarorum in Romanum ſo-
lum armati venerunt.
Trebellius Pollio de Divo Claudio, § 7.

Claudius Boccho, delevimus trecenta viginta millia
Gothorum, duo milia navium merſimus. § 8.

h

he wrote to the fenate before the action,
and after it to Bocchus, that we learn
the numbers of the army, and of the
fleet. The firft he reprefents as confifting of 320,000 men in arms; and
the latter as of 2000 fhips. Although
hiftory does not here, as in the Baltic,
afford any account of the origin and progrefs of this power; yet in thefe inftances
we fee the ufe and effect of it. It feems
not to be known till its power was felt.
In like manner, in the firft account of
negotiations which the Romans had with
the Jazyges on the Danube, one article of
the peace was, that they fhould not ufe
their own fhips on the Danube, nor make
fettlements on the iflands therein.

The famous cruizing voyage made by
the Franks is not only an inftance but a
proof of the fpirit of enterprize, and very
advanced progrefs, of the navigation and
naval power of thefe people in that early
period. They failed from the Euxine
fea through the Mediterranean, and, paffing the ftraights of Gibraltar, coafted the
whole Weftern fhores of Europe, till they
arrived on the Saxon fhores. In the courfe
of this voyage they made various prædatory incurfions upon the coafts of Afia
and

and Greece; they attempted the same, but not with success, on the coasts of Africa : however they surprized Sicily, and made great prey at Syracuse.

The navigators of the Baltic and-Saxon shores were, as we have seen, themselves the warriors. The navigators of the Euxine, and waters of the great rivers which fell into it, were not so. Yet, when by the fate of war they became subject, or by the bonds of treaty, were united in service to the warrior nations, that power, by the union of the two, was formed, which the Roman arms could never effectually repress : to which power the emperors became tributary, purchasing peace of these invaders by annual payments. Caracalla thus bought peace of the naval people of the Northern Ocean ; as did Gallus of the Goths upon the Danube. But neither arms nor money could restrain the course of this increasing and ascendant power, which finally bore down all before it, even the seat of the empire itself.

The two great rivers, the Rhine and the Danube were the two avenues, the one from the Northern Ocean, the other from

from the Euxine fea, to the very confines
of Italy. And accordingly, in the vales
of thefe rivers, on their banks, and on
their waters, were the invaders of the
Roman empire always found; as were
the battles fought which decided the fate
of it.

The experienced wifdom and grounded
policy of Auguftus confidered * thefe
rivers as proper boundaries of the empire;
and the command of them as its defence;
for, by means of thefe, the regions, provinces, fleets, and whole power of the
empire, might have a connected fyftem.
When the Roman emperors, quitting
this wife fyftem, endeavoured to extend
the empire by more advanced and more
enlarged bounds, they found that they
opened their flanks, lefs connected and
lefs defentible, in any given point : and
expofed to an enemy who was able to
bring its whole force to the point of attack. The lines of defence of the frontiers

* Cuncta fua manu confcripferat Auguftus. Addiderat-
que confilium, coercendi inter terminos imperii, Taciti
Ann. lib. I. § 11.—Mari Oceano, aut amnibus longinquis
feptum imperium, regiones, provincias, claffes, cuncta inter
fe connexa. Taciti Annales, lib. I. § 9.

not

not only diverged, but became unconnected; while the lines of attack of the enemy converged to, and were united in, the point where they acted on the offensive.

This matter of the relative numbers and force, which these invaders on one hand, and the empire on the other, could bring into the field against each other, seems to want some farther investigation, and explanation. The Roman empire had certainly not only great numbers of people, but more numerous armies; armies more highly disciplined; as also an absolute command of all those resources which support armies, and enable them to act; beyond what the enemy could possibly possess. Yet these invading Barbarians, as they are called, seem always to have advanced with numbers, which exceeded the number of the armies which the Roman frontiers opposed to them; and generally to be superior in the efforts of force with which they attacked.

We have seen above, that the whole nation of these uncivilized people wore arms; and that a fourth part at least was their actual army, effective and under arms.

arms. A policied nation, whofe community is divided and diftributed into various and multiplied departments of em-
ployment and fervice; who neceffarily
muft have many orders and defcriptions
of people exempt from bearing arms;
who, as many of the orders of the ftate,
as well as the army, are unprodu&tive towards the fupply, muft have a great proportion of the people of the community employed in the produ&tion of food,
in the manufa&ture, cloathing, habitation, arms and implements of war; in
the mechanic arts, in carriage, and diftribution. A policied nation, who muft
have a numerous magiftracy, a priefthood,
multitudes of officers of police, multitudes
of officers of revenue; and who hath alfo
naturally, multitudes of idle, non-effi-
cient, unprodu&tive hands, employed
only in wafte, in the parade of vanity,
and in fubminiftration to luxury and vice;
a nation, whofe refources of revenue are
perverted and wafted, could not maintain, even if they could raife, more than
a defined number of troops, proportioned
to the defalcated furplus of their fupply
and finances. A nation in fuch a ftate,
and arrived at fuch a degree in the progreffion of civilization, never could maintain

5   (as

(as the eftimation of political calculators
reckon) more than one in every hundredth
part of its people as an *eftablifhed* army * ;
fo that the numbers, which a nation in
that inferior advance of civilization, under
which we have defcribed the invaders of
the Roman dominions to be, can bring

* Take an exifting example in modern times. People
uninformed in thefe matters, and unexperienced in practice, are difappointed in their calculations, and wonder
with aftonifhment that the French can now raife fo many
armies, and bring fuch effective numbers into the field,
beyond any proportion of numbers which the old French
Government could produce. But if we confider them,
under their prefent ftate of diforganization, as this treatife
hath defcribed the ftate of the nations which invaded Rome,
the wonder will ceafe, and the fact be feen as the natural
effect of caufes operating on the nature of man.

Have fuch wonderers already forgotten what fucceffive
numbers, year after year, the Americans brought into the
field, maintaining and fupporting them at one thoufandth,
one may fay at one millionth, part of the expence which
the European armies fent againft them coft.

✓ The fubjugation of the Americans was known at that
time, to fuch as knew them on experience, to be impracticable : fo would the combined efforts of all the powers of
Europe allied againft the French prove, had thefe people
the prudence, the practical knowledge, and political virtue, which the Americans exhibited, in forming, or
rather following, fome actual fyftem of Government. If
the horrid, felf-deftructive, functions of the French, which
prey upon their vitals, do not conquer them internally,
they will not be conquered from without.

This modern example is an illuftration of former facts ;
and the reafoning by which former facts are explained might
with ufe be directly applied, on the grounds of experience,
to the acting towards the prefent cafe here ftated.

into

into the field, exceeds, *cæteris paribus*, the numbers which a *policied* nation can raife and maintain as a ftanding army, in the proportion of twenty-five to one, and of one hundred to one in the cafe of defenfive fervice. I have faid *cæteris paribus*, meaning if the total of the numbers of the nations were equal. But the fuperior total of the numbers of the Roman empire balanced this proportion nearer to an equipoife. And fo long as the frontiers of the Roman dominions could be attacked on one point only, at one time, as their frontiers on the Rhine for inftance, or on the Danube, the fuperior numbers armed and trained, which the Roman government had in its fervice, and could bring to thefe points, did render, and muft always have rendered, thofe frontiers impregnable, as to any impreffion to be made by any general irruption. * Nothing, however, at the fame time, except *continued lines* of defence, like the Chinefe wall, along the whole extent of thefe frontiers, could

---

* I am juftified in forming and giving this opinion when the fact turns out, that Hadrian firft drew fuch lines from the Danube to the Rhine, which Probus afterward formed into a regular fortification by a ftone-wall flanked with towers; when alfo Agricola and Severus built a like defence againft the Scots and Picts acrofs the ifland of Britain.

guard

guard againſt temporary inroads and
partial irruptions of flying armies of this
prædatory enemy; who were from the
forms and habits of their life, always prepared to make and were perpetually making, deſtructive inroads, or prædatory in-
vaſions on the provinces. When the frontiers of the dominions were extended in
an immenſe circular unconnected periphery
along the mountain Atlas in Africa to
Ægypt; acroſs that vale, and the deſerts of
Arabia; thence along the Eaſtern parts of
Syria, and Aſia, into the Parthian country,
and ſo round North by the Caſpian and
Euxine ſeas; and thence along the vales of
the Dneiſter, the Danube, and Rhine; and
over the fortified intervals of land which
lay between them; and along the coaſts
and rivers of the Northern Sea, and Atlantic Ocean: And when invading enemies, ſuch in numbers, and of ſuch active force as hath been deſcribed, animated
with unconquerable though not undiſci-
plined ſpirit, recoiled upon this conquer-
ing empire, and attacked theſe frontiers
in almoſt every point, with a naval force on
the Eaſtern and Weſtern coaſts, up the
waters of the Danube and the Rhine, and
up thoſe of Gaul; when Saxons, Goths,
Vandals, Franks, &c. &c. advanced upon
the

the Weſt and South-Weſt; Germans, Alemans, Burgundians, &c. on the North; Goths, Hunns, and Alanns, on the North-Eaſt; Parthians on the Eaſt; and Saracens on the South and South-Eaſt; the forces of the empire which became neceſſary in every part that was liable to attack, in every point of time, were, howſoever numerous they were upon the whole, hardly equal in any part, and in many parts unequal to the force with which they were invaded. It was not only that the union of their ſyſtem of force was thus divided; but the ſervices and commands of the empire were ſeparated and independent of each other. They then became not only jealous of, but interfered with, each other. Theſe ſeparate commands engaged in the conteſts, which the different factious claims to the empire created; and were generally in oppoſition to, if not in open war with, one another; and by engaging and employing the force of the barbarous nations againſt the Romans in theſe alternate conteſts, they even trained them to conqueſt over the Roman empire itſelf. Circumſtances in the natural courſe of events led to the dividing of the dominions of the empire into Eaſt and Weſt; and finally,

N　　　　　　　in

in the political courfe of events, to the removing of the feat of empire from Rome to Conftantinople.

Hiftorians and politicians hold various opinions on the effect of this event: whether this did, or did not, leave the Weftern and Roman Empire, originally fo called, as alfo the old feat of Empire, Rome, open on its flanks, and ftripped of half its force, at a time when the whole was hardly equal to its defence; and thus expofed to enemies which came upon it in all directions; and finally deftroyed it.

The antiquary, as the mere commentator on hiftory, without prefuming to be a politician, will difcover, that, as the Weftern Ocean, the Rhine, and the rivers of Gaul on one part, and the Danube, on the other, were the great avenues from the Weft, the North, and North-Eaft, to the very gates of Italy, the Roman provinces of the Weftern Empire were thus left in one flank wholly undefended, in front but half defended, and on the other flank wholly abandoned. The powers, fuch as have been defcribed, both naval and landed, muft muſt force their way in every line and point of attack. He will ſee the great aſcendant naval power of the Saxons, Goths, Danes, and Franks, ravaging the Weſtern coaſts; and penetrating, in conjunction with the land forces, into all the Weſtern provinces. He will find them in Spain, in Africa, and from Africa, advancing to Rome. He will find Goths, Vandals, Alemanns, Burgundians on the Rhine; Alemanns, Goths, Sarmatians, Hunns, and Alanns, on the Danube; and advancing up theſe great avenues ſo as to penetrate Italy. He will view this diviſion of the empire, and this removal of the ſeat of empire to Conſtantinople, as the *external fundamental* cauſe of the diſſolution and deſtruction of the Weſtern or Roman Empire, whatever *inſtrumental* cauſes, internal as well as external, operated to that effect in future events.

The antiquary perhaps may be able to collect, that, even in the time of Auguſtus, ſpeculations were floating on the waves of popular opinion, as to the policy of eſtabliſhing a ſecondary metropolis, or ſeat of empire, in Aſia, ſomewhere near the Boſphorus; and that adulation to the Julian family fixed on the ſcite of

old

old Ilium for the place. This fuppofition not only explains, but illuftrates,
one of the fineft odes which Horace wrote;
I mean the third of the third book. This
ode appears to have been written in direct
purpofe to obviate the dangerous tendency
of fuch political theorems, fo contrary to
the fpirit and prudence of Auguftus's
fyftem. The antiquary will fee with what
fine addrefs thefe political fpeculations are
met; and with what art the adulation is
repreffed, without being reprobated. The
ode opens with a maxim, that the juft and
determined man muft not be moved with
the falfe ardor of the people calling for
wrong meafures: that he will fix his plan
in truth and right; and will be decided by
the principles of that alone. He defcribes
this fpirit of character to be that which
placed the antient heroes amongft the
Gods; amongft whom alfo he places Auguftus. The ode then takes for its foundation the fpeech of Juno to Neptune, in
the 20th book of the Iliad:

310 Ἐννοσίγαι᾽, αὐτὸς σὺ μεῖὰ φρεσὶ σῇσι νόησον
     Αἰνείαν, ἥκεν μὶν ἐρύσσεαι, ἥκεν ἐάσῃς
     Πηλείδη Ἀχιλῆϊ δαμήμεναι, ἐσθλὸν ἐόν]α·
     Ἦτοι μὲν γὰρ Νῶϊ πολεῖς ὡρμασσαμεν ὅρκους
     Πᾶσι μεῖ᾽ Ἀθανάτοισι Ἐγὼ ϰ Παλλὰς Ἀθήνη
                                        Μήποῖ᾽

Μήποτ' ἐπὶ Τρώεσσιν ἀλεξήσειν κακὸν ἦμαρ,
Μηδ' ὁπόταν Τροίη μαλερῷ πυρὶ πᾶσα δαίηται.

Good as he is, to immolate or fpare
The Dardan prince, O Neptune, be thy
    care.
Pallas and I, by all that Gods can bind,
Have fworn deftruction to the Trojan
    kind ;
Not e'en an inftant to protract their fate ;
Or fave one member of the finking ftate,
'Till her laft flame be quench'd with her
    laft gore,
And e'en her crumbling ruins are no
    more.   Pope.

    This fpeech was an anfwer to what
Neptune had faid about the prefervation
of Æneas, whom fate had fixed to be the
author of a race who fhould reign over
men to all generations. " Be that as it
may," fays Juno; " and be it your care to
fave Æneas ; but the deftiny of the kingdom of Troy is, that it is to be ruined,
and fhall never more arife unlefs to experience a like repeated fate." On this
decree and deftiny of Heaven, thus pro-
phetically denounced, as a religious truth,

          againft

againſt which theſe ſpeculations are by
the poet repreſented as riſing in defiance,
he founds his ode; which is a paraphraſe
of Juno's ſpeech.

P. 37.   Dum longus inter ſæviat Ilion
          Romanaque Pontus, quâlibet exſules
          In parte regnanto beati.

P. 53.   Quicunque mundo terminus ob-
                ſtitit,
          Hunc tangat armis, viſere geſtiens,
          Quâ parte debacchantur ignes.
              Quâ nebulæ pluviique rores.

Sed bellicoſis fata Quiritibus,
Hac lege dico, *ne nimium pii*
    Rebuſque fidentes, avitæ
        Tecta velint reparare Trojæ.

Trojæ renaſcens alite lugubri
Fortuna triſti clade iterabitur,
    Ducente victrices catervas
        Conjuge me Jovis, et ſorore.

Obſerve here how delicately the ſentiments
in which the adulation was conveyed, is
touched and repreſſed; as, *nimium pii—
Rebuſque fidentes.*

This

This is, I fear, rather a digreſſion ; but the matter comes up ſo fully to the ſentiment, which I had ventured to ſuggeſt on the ſubject of the removal of the ſeat of empire ; and points out ſo clearly what were the ſentiments of Auguſtus and his miniſter on the ſame ſubject, that I hope as an antiquary I may be excuſed. I would venture further to ſay, that placing this fine ode in this point of view, places it in its true light, and gives the beſt illuſtration of it : and thus the antiquary becomes a critic.

If the learned antiquary ſhall examine the great event, the total change of the inhabitancy of the civilized parts of Europe, in ſome ſuch line of inveſtigation as hath been, by this treatiſe, in a very ſuperficial and imperfect manner, ſketched out ; if he ſhall conſider, by facts and principles combined, in ſome ſuch manner as hath been ſuggeſted herein above, the nature of the population of the human ſpecies, in the various gradations of its humanization and civilization ; he will clearly ſee how, at that period of this great revolution, theſe half humanized clans and hords of the North, having coaleſced into approximations by ſo-

ciety,

ciety, and being in a progreffive ftate towards civilization, became, in that ftage of their being, populous beyond what they ever were before, and beyond what the fame will ever be again. He will fee how in that ftage of their progreffion, they retaining their war-principles, and being formed not into a policied ftate, but into a national army, muft have been in force equal to their numbers. When he fees this nation, as an united, locomotive, active body, living and moving as an army; and in all its movements and pofitions, in perfect command of its fupply; he will view this great revolution, effected by thefe people, in a very different light from that in which it hath been commonly placed and viewed.

If the antiquary, having thus examined the caufes, looks to the effect, which this general revolution muft have had, and actually had; tracing that effect in the manners of thefe new lords of the world; he will find that he has acquired a plain clue to that labyrinth, which learning had rendered fo perplexed.

Of the *two great characteriftic lines* of the new eftablifhment, one was, the *feudal*

dal state of the property *of the land*, and of the military *service of the person:* the other was the almoft total difregard in which they held the civil-conftitutions, as mere matter of home œconomy.

The antiquary has feen already explained, the manner in which the *principes* of the ftate were furrounded with attendant military *comites or ambacles;* pledged in the ftrongeft *perfonal fealty* to their feryice : as alfo how thefe *principes* diftributed to thefe their military followers, fuch *beneficia* as their prædatory booty, or the fpoils of war, enabled them to give.

The antiquary will alfo have read, in the cafe of the *Cimbri* *, (as an inftance,) that the people had a diftinct idea of *holding lands* from the donor as a ftipendium, *on tenure of military fervice*. If he combines this idea with that of the community being divided into † *principes*, and

---

* Cimbri et Teutones mifere legatos in caftra Silani, inde ad fenatum, petentes, ut *Martius Populus* aliquid, fibi terræ daret, quafi ftipendium, cæterum ut vellet manibus et armis fuis uteretur.

L. Ann. Florus, lib. III. chap. 3.

† Cæfar de Bell. Gall. lib. VI. § 14.

I   their

their *clientes*, *ambactos*, or *comites*; he will derive, from thefe cuftoms of thefe people, the *origin*, not only *of fealty* in general, but of the *landed feudal* conftitution, and of *property held quafi ftipendium.* * If after thefe he examines, as foon as he finds an inftance, how the Romans arranged the fervice of their frontiers, he will find them creating a like fealty, and a very fimilar feudal tenure of land in thefe parts, the lands of which Tacitus calls *Decumatos agros*, a tenure well known and eftablifhed in his time. They had been long in the ufage of letting the conquered lands on a † tithe-rent. Here they divided their lands into military benefices, *quafi ftipendia*, the lands were called *agri limitanei*, and the officers and

---

* Sola, quæ de hoftibus capta funt, limitaneis ducibus et militibus donavit, ita, ut eorum ita effent, fi hæredes eorum militarent, nec unquam ad privatos pertinerent: dicens, attentiùs eos militaturos fi etiam fua rura detenderent. This is faid of Alexander Severus.

Lampridius, in Alexan. chap. 58.

Veteranis omnia illa, quæ angufta adeunt Ifauriæ loca, privatis [Probus] donavit, addens, ut eorum filii ab anno octavo decimo mares duntaxat ab militiam mitterentur.

Vopifcus, chap. 16.

† Omnis ager Siciliæ decu manus eft.

Cicero in Verr.

foldiers

foldiers to whom they were granted were denominated *duces et milites limitanei*. The *ufu fruĉtus* was in the military tenant, on the condition of his ferving in the armies on the frontiers; but the dominion and property remained in the ftate, and never could become private property. The heirs of thefe military tenants, if, after their fathers death, or at their coming to the age of eighteen, they took their fathers place in the fervice, fucceeded to thefe *beneficia*, but not otherwife. This inftitution of a landed military, as a regulation of the defence of the frontiers, grew into a conftitution of ftate. The Northern conquerors, when they mounted to the feat of empire, found their own ufage and fyftem perhaps more regularly arranged in practice; and it became a *fundamental eftablifhment of their* IMPERIUM.

The antiquary will have feen that, befides this, there were amongft thefe people other bafe tenures, particularly that of foccage and menial fervices, prior to their conqueft of the empire. Their vaffals or flaves held lands under the tenure of paying a certain portion of corn and grain, cattle and cloathing.

Thefe

These sources of men, with maintenance for their armies, together with the tribute which the conquerors affessed and levied, being thus provided for, they no more regarded nor entered into the administration of the political government than they would have entered into the house of œconomy: they held both equally below the tour of duty of a warrior. They frequently appointed the very kings, or other governors, whom they had conquered, to the government of their own kingdoms, under the tenure of paying tribute, and supplying recruits to the army; and as responsible for the obedience of the state. At other times these conquerors and commanders, according to a custom which the antiquary will have seen frequently take place, made a partition of the government, taking themselves the command of the force of it, of the army and navy; and leaving as a subordinated department, the administration of the polity, œconomy, and justice, to the regulus, the inferior king, as an office under them. At other times they appointed some of the kings or governors of other countries which they had subdued, and whom perhaps they had taken in battle; of which there are many instances. Whole
nations

nations (fays Dr. Mafcou *, fpecifying particular cafes) fubmitted themfelves to the Franks, or rather only to the King, putting themfelves in fealty to him, but retaining their conftitution, liberties, and laws. The Dukes of Aquitain, Bavaria, and Swabia, did this. The Lombards alfo did the fame, but under particular regulated conditions, fuited to the circumftances of their government; likewife the Wifgoths and Burgundians. I believe he will feldom find them appointing any of their own principal officers, as thefe political commands were always confidered, not only as fubordinate to the military, but below the tour of duty which it was fit for a military officer to hold.

From this fpirit of their confidering the political conftitutions and adminiftration as merely œconomical, on which the power of the fupreme command no ways depended, may be derived the reafon of their kingdoms being divided into fo

* Hift. of the Germans, lib. XVI. § 39; alfo N° 35 and 36 of the Annotations, alfo Annot 26, and Annot. ;.— This book, befides being a very learned and very ingenious compilation, and a commentary on the ancient hiftory of the Germans, grounded in real knowledge, is a perfect Bibliotheque on that fubject, as more writers, than are willing to own their obligations to it, have found.

many

many diftinct polities; and as the fource of fo many, and fuch various, curiæ and jurifdictions, laws and cuftoms. Here the antiquary will have feen, in the original habits of thefe people, that the dividing the general empire into feveral domains, each having, within its refpective jurifdiction, an independent internal political imperium, was a meafure in the natural courfe of their fyftem, and did no ways interrupt or interfere with the general paramount command, which they held over the countries that they conquered. In thefe cuftoms he will fee the origin of thofe great palatine offices in the ftate; and the fource of their growing by degrees to fupreme; and thence, in the courfe of events, to ufurping the exercife of the fovereign power : and finally of their becoming abfolutely fovereign. This was the cafe of the great officer of the Mayor of the Palace, and of all other palatines, having the prerogatives of a palace as a feat of government. From this general fource, and in thefe two lines of derivation may be traced the foundation of all the governments in Europe, (thofe in the Baltic and that of Britain excepted,) which came into fovereign eftablifhment on the decline, and at the diffolution, of the general empire of the Franks.

From

From the fame fource, and in the fame lines of derivation, may be traced the reafon why there were fo many and fuch different civil jurifdictions and curiæ, diftinct and independent of each other. The foregoing ftate of the police of thefe people explains how all this was confiftent with the adminiftration of their government, fo long as all were under fealty which concentered to the power of the Paramount and Sovereign Lord.

To the fpirit of this fyftem of government is to be imputed the turn of the laws of treafon. The political government and community, being not only feparated from the fovereignty, but being confidered by the fovereign as a mere fubordinate matter of adminiftration fcarce worth his attention, the crime of treafon took place only by acts againft the fovereign : and was indicted and punifhed only in that predicament. From this mode alfo of confidering the perfons of the nation, not under the idea of members of a community living under and entitled to perfonal rights ; but, as the king's foldiers and fubjects, members of his military imperium ; all offences and injuries, committed upon the fubject or his feudum, were,

were, upon the fuppofition * that the fovereign was thereby injured, either by the
lofs of his foldier, or by that foldier being
rendered in his perfon, or in his poffeffion,
incapable, or at leaft lefs capable, of ferving his Lord according to his engagement,
profecuted or indicted as offences againft
the fovereign, and not under the idea of
doing juftice to the individual, on the
ground of his claim to protection in his
own right.

The antiquary might, in like manner,
trace the ground of all the alterations,
which this feudal fyftem of government,
when it became eftablifhed in all its rigors
under hereditary monarchs, made in the
conftitution of thofe ftates wherein the
*falus populi (et non Domini) fuprema lex
fuerat.*

But thefe are fubjects which may be
thought more proper for the confideration
of the lawyer or ftatefman than the antiquary. And as, although I think it the
duty of every freeman to underftand the
laws of a ftate of which he is a member,
I do not pretume to be a lawyer, I will
here ceafe *Magna modis tenuare parvis.*

* Læfa aut imminuta majeftas.

After

After a general review of this great revolution in the inhabitancy and government of Europe, analyfed in its caufe,
and traced in its effects, to the general
eftablifhment of the new fyftem, in fome
fuch lines as have been here fuggefted and
fketched out ; the antiquary of each
country may take his own peculiar courfe
of enquiry into the antient ftate and operations of his own nation and government.

O   R E-

Remarks on fome Criticifms made by the Rev. Mr. Whitaker, on two or three Parts of Governor Pownall's Book, intituled, " No= " tices of Antiquities remaining " in the Provincia Romana of " Gaul."

Mr. WHITAKER, in a late ingenious and learned work which he has pub-lifhed, entituled, " The Courfe of Hau- " nibal over the Alps afcertained," has thought it worth his while to go out of his way to exercife his criticifm on fome parts of my notices, which were pub-lifhed not for the information of fuch la-borioufly learned men as Mr. Whitaker, but for the ufe and amufement of fuch defultory readers, and fuch idle travellers as myfelf. However, as I wifh to be ac-curate even in trifles; and not to be mif-

appre-

apprehended or mifreprefented, even in the humble character of an author, I will endeavour to juftify my Notices; ftating them to be as they are, however infignificant they may be.

This lively gentleman is pleafed (vol. I. p. 37.) to flatter me in a manner which I neither defire nor deferve; that I have defcribed the Triumphal Arch at Orange with ingenuity and judgement; yet, at the fame time, fays, " that I have " thought without accuracy, and con- " cluded without evidence; that the " paffages which I have quoted from " Strabo in confirmation of my opinion, " concerning the origin of this arch, de- " ftroy all I have written about it." He then * confounding two very different things as the fame, fc. trophies [Trophæal Monument and Saxeæ Turres,] and triumphal arches, fays, " that thefe mo- " numents (fc. Trophæal) could not, " (common fenfe forbids it,) be fixed on " the field of battle, the open heath, or " bleak mountains, on which the bat-

---

* This is a favourite expreffion with Mr. Whitaker; be that my apology for ufing fo uncivil a term to a learned and reverend gentleman.

" tles

" tles were fought, notwithſtanding what
" Strabo and Florus ſeem to inſinuate ;
" and as all our writers have taken for
" granted from them." This is an argu-
ment *à priori* ſet againſt *faɛt*. The faɛt
is, that theſe trophies, and trophæal monuments, were aɛtually ſet up on the
field of battle, *in loco pugnæ*, and on the
bleak mountains. *Pompeius de viɛtis Hiſ-
panis Trophæa in Pyreneis jugis conſtituit,*
Salluſtii fragmenta, Ap. Serv. whilſt
triumphal arches were, as I have explained and diſtinguiſhed them, ereɛted
in the very ſituations which this gentleman fixes upon for trophies or trophæal
monuments.

If I had thought, as he ſtates me to
have thought, or had concluded, as he
concludes for me, he certainly would
have been founded in his criticiſm : but
if any poor opinion of mine was ſo far
worth his notice, that it could have ar-
reſted for a moment the quickneſs of his
conception, and the rapidity of his pen,
he would have ſeen with what an endeavour at accuracy (in pages 36, 7, 8) I
have diſtinguiſhed trophæal monuments,
ereɛted on the fields of battle by the generals and their armies, from triumphal

O 3   arches

arches, erected by the authority of government, after thefe generals had been
admitted to the honour of a triumph. He
would have feen, that although I fuppofe
the triumphal arch at Orange to have
been erected to the honour of Fabius
Maximus, and in commemoration of his
victory gained near the Ifar ; yet I ftate
both Fabius Maximus, and Dom. Ænobarbus, to have erected diftinct trophies,
each his refpective monument on his own
refpective field of battle; and I quote
Strabo to this point, and not to the point
which Mr. Witaker miftakes and mif-
ftates. Although I fay, which Strabo, as
quoted by me, confirms, that each built
his trophæal monument on his refpective
field of battle; " Yet, I fay, that thefe
" ftone towers, fo built by the generals
" and their armies, could only be tro-
" phæal monuments; in that no one
" could prefume to erect a triumphal
" arch but by authority of government,
" after he had obtained the honour of a
" triumph."

If this gentleman, inftead of imputing
want of accuracy to me, had read thefe
paffages with *his* ufual accuracy, he
would have fpared the criticifm which
he

he made, " that I had thought without
" accuracy ; and had made quotations of
" facts which deftroy all I had written
" about the origin of this triumphal
" arch." If he. had applied his ufual
acutenefs of judgement to the reafons
which I give why this could not be referred to Ænobarbus *, and to thofe
which induce me to conclude that it was
erected to Fabius Maximus, I dare vouch
for his candour, that he would not have
faid that I conclude without evidence.
I do believe that he would allow that the
conclufion was fairly drawn, although I
do not affume *to afcertain*; I go no farther than conjecture, (p. 39.)

NUMBER II.

In a fubfequent note (vol. I. p. 87.) of
this work, Mr. Whitaker laments that
the unwelcome lot of diffecting and ex-
hibiting a fignal inftance of my *geographical confufednefs* has fallen to him ;

* I much doubt whether any triumphal arch was ever
erected to Dom. Ænobarbus.

yet,

yet, in the doing of this, *haud fuaviter in modo*, he affumes an air of fuperiority in a language ufed only by fchool-mafters towards their fchool-boys. However, I confole myfelf with being affured, that the reprehending and correcting language which he ufes arifes more from habit in the manner and ftyle than from his temper and fpirit; as I find others (Polybius and Livy efpecially) exhibited, diffected, and corrected, in the fame manner and ftyle of criticifm, whenever their geography or defcriptions differ from his; although they are perhaps defcribing very different places, or very different circumftances, from thofe which this gentleman has preconceived. I will put a few famples in a note below *.

My

---

* Whitaker, vol. I. p. 126. Yet Livy, with that indiftinctnefs of geographical vifion, which begins here to perplex his hiftorical views; and which appears overfetting his hiftorical ideas hereafter, defcribes Hannibal, at this point, as turning to the left.

P. 127. Livy was not aware of his own contradictions, he did not know that his remarks were confuted by his facts.

P. 204. Livy hardly knows the juft meaning of his words.

P. 300. Livy's affertion, that the Veragri were inhabitants of the Pennine Alps, is a ftrong evidence of what I have noted before, his unfkilfulnefs in the general geography of the regions through which he had been hitherto conducting Hannibal.

P. 361,

My offence is, the " being of opinion
" with thofe learned antiquaries, who
" have,

P. 361. So very unfkilful is Livy in the very incidents
of his own period! fo treacherous in his memory, or fo
imperfect in his notices, even of the moft recent and moft
public events.

P. 362. So much does Strabo vie in contradictorinefs
and confufion with Livy.

P. 374. Never, fure, was a writer more completely
confuted than Livy thus is by his own facts; he falls upon
his own fword; he dies by his own hands.

Vol. II. p. 97. The truth is, Livy in the former paffage has confounded the Libui and Cenomanni together,
&c. We fee alfo Livy bringing over the Salluvii of Mar-
feille where he had juft fixed the Cenomanni before; fo
corrects the miftake without knowing it; and adds a contradiction to the error without being confcious of it.

P. 231. With fo much confufion in circumftances do
both Polybius and Livy conclude their account of Hannibal's march. Yet the reader will remember and obferve,
that Polybius had not only taken his account from people living on the fpot at the time, but had hisfelf gone exprefsly to examine the *Local*.

Vol. I. p. 129. This inftance of inaccuracy in Polybius forms a parallel to the other in Livy; and is indeed
more culpable in Polybius, than the other is in Livy, becaufe the former travelled into Gaul, and *feems to have vi-
fited Lyons*, for the fake of local information. This fhews
the advantage which *we moderns* have over the ancients by
the help of maps.

P. 168. All that march however of Hannibal, though
it was purfued through *a couple of nations* is totally omitted
by Polybius.

Q. Was the march of Hannibal, according to Polybius,
conducted through *that couple of nations?*

P. 171. Mr. de St. Simon obferved that Polybius carried
Hannibal over the Druentia, and (as he fhould alfo have obferved) carried him by a road, moftly level, to the Alps.
But Polybius had lept over this intermediate region, and
therefore he and Folard refufed to pace over it. Q. Whether

" have, with a great degree of probabi-
" lity, traced the march of Hannibal
" through this vale:" and merely becaufe I fay, " It became matter of amufe-
" ment whilft paffing down from the
" heights of Montlimart, to trace and
" follow with my eye the *fuppofed courfe*
" of this march, as Hannibal is *fuppofed*
" to have paffed the Rhone at Beaucare
" and Roquemaure; to have marched in
" two columns up to Ambrone; and to

ther Mr. Whitaker and thefe authors are not at crofs-pur-
pofes, defcribing a very different rout, over a very different
river from that which he fuppofes to be the Druentia?
Vol. II. p. 45. The Alps (obferves Polybius) on their
tops, and on the parts adjoining to the paffes, are all perfectly bare of trees, and naked of themfelves, becaufe the
fnow lies on them continually, both winter and fummer.
This account, however, fays Mr. Whitaker, is confufed,
exaggerated, and falfe. Q. Did Polybius, by the words
'Αλπιων ακρα, mean the fame thing as Mr. Whitaker's tops?
The confufion lies with him who takes two different things
to be the fame. It certainly is not true, and would be an
exaggerated account, to fay that the tops of the Alps in general are continually covered with fnow; but it is certainly
true, and no exaggeration, to fay, the "Ακρα, the higheft
extreme points, as Mont Blanc for inftance, is continually
covered with fnow.
To clofe this note, I will refer to a general remark, made
by Mr. Whitaker, on all the delineators of Hannibal's
march, prior to *his* undertaking *to afcertain it:* chap.
III. § 5. p. 248. We are now come to that point of
Hannibal's march which none of the delineators of his
march have prefumed to touch. They have all agreed in
one general confpiracy againft the facts, that now fuc-
ceed immediately in his hiftory; and have united to fup-
prefs them entirely.

5

" have

" have thence pierced through the paſſes
" (thoſe of the white rock) of the Celtic
" Alps"—[Although I uſe the ¡general
appellation Celtic Alpes, diſtinguiſhing
theſe parts from Maritime Alpes, yet Mr.
Whitaker acknowledges that I was not
ignorant that theſe parts, by a ſpecial
diviſion, were called the Cottian Alps,]
— " ſo confounded," ſays Mr. Whitaker, " does Mr. Pownall appear in the
" geography of the very country he is
" viſiting." Here this gentleman ſuppoſes me to ſuppoſe, that Roquemaure,
and not Taraſcon, is oppoſite to Reau-
caire; and to be ignorant that Roquemaure is many miles higher up the river;
on the contrary, the account which I give
that Hannibal paſſed his army over at theſe
two places is founded in faċt *. That
when he was preparing to paſs his main-

---

* Jamque omnibus fatis comparatis ad trajiciendum,
terrebant ex adverſo hoſtes, omnem ripam equites virique
obtinentes; quos ut averteret, Hannonem, Bomilcaris filium
vigilià primà noċtis, cum parte copiarum, maxime Hiſpa-
nis, adverſo flumine, ire iter unius diei jubet. Et ubi primum poteſt, quam occultiſſimè, trajeċto amni, circumdu-
cere agmen, ut, cum opus faċto ſit, adoriatur a tergo hoſ-
tem, ad id dati duces Gaili educunt inde millia quinque et
viginti firmè ſuprà parvæ inſulæ circumfuſum amnem, &c.
N. B. This account given by Livy is almoſt literally tranſlated from Polybius.

body

body over at Beaucaire, he fent up on the Weft fide of the river a detachment commanded by Hanno, with orders to pafs the river, at about a day's march diftant, fo as to come upon the rear of the enemy, who oppofed themfelves to him on the oppofite bank of the river. That this detachment went on this rout twenty-five miles, and croffed the river, at a place fo precifely and fpecifically defcribed by Livy*, that it is impoffible to miftake it, and not to fix upon the fpot. Roquemaure is about twenty-five miles diftant from Beaucaire ; and is, as to the *local*, juft as Polybius and Livy defcribe it.

As foon as Hannibal knew, from a fignal made by Hanno, that this detachment had paffed, he began to tranfport his main body over. The enemy oppofed him ; but Hanno, with his detachment, came down upon their rear. They took the alarm, and quitted the conteft. Hannibal then paffed the remainder over without any oppofition.

---

* To ufe the words of Mr. Whitaker, " faithful to " reality even in the minuteft touches of his pencil." Livy, as may be feen above, is not always fo fortunate as to have the good opinion of this gentleman.

Mr.

Mr. Whitaker hisfelf takes notice (vol. I. 190) of this detachment paffing the river, at fome place above the main body, &c. And yet has this gentleman fo confounded* himfelf, by preconceived notions, not only in the geography of the country, but alfo in the movement of an army whofe courfe of march he is defcribing, that the reference which I make to *two trajects* appears to him all confufion of fact and ignorance of geography. On the contrary, my fixing upon Roquemaure for the traject at which Hanno's detachment paffed the river, whilft Hannibal was preparing to pafs at Beaucaire, is, I would hope, founded in fome geographical knowledge of the country I was vifiting.

As I am not writing the hiftory of this march, but only amufing myfelf with tracing by my eye the *fuppofed courfe* of it, according to the opinion of others. It is not now, any more than it was then neceffary to go into a detail of it. I will however ftate one reafon, added to thofe whereon many learned antiquaries had founded their opinion of the army march-

* A favorite expreffion with Mr. Whitaker.

ing

ing to Ambrone, which induced me to
adopt this their opinion.

Polybius exprefsly fays, that as foon as
Hannibal had paffed the Rhone, he formed
his line of march; placing his cavalry and
elephants in the rear, next the river, * $\varpi\alpha\rho\grave{\alpha}$
$\tau\grave{o}\nu$ $\varpi o\tau\alpha\mu\grave{o}\nu$, thence took his rout † in a
courfe from the fea one while going eaft-
ward, one while towards the midland
country of Europe; now the combined
line of this courfe would be E. N. E. and
lead to Ambrone.

This courfe in that direction of it which
went *Eaft* could not " keep clofe to the
" Rhone," as Mr. Whitaker defcribes it:
the courfe up the Rhone is direct North.
Polybius could not be, nor can he, by
any ingenuity, be fuppofed to be ignorant,
that the courfe up the river was North;
nor would he, if he fuppofed Hannibal to
keep clofe to the Rhone, defcribe the
courfe of his march in any part of it $\epsilon\iota\varsigma$
$\tau\tilde{\eta}\nu$ $\check{\epsilon}\omega$.

---

* Πα$\varrho\grave{\alpha}$ with an accufative cafe in this conftruction im-
ports juxtà, $\varpi\alpha\rho\grave{\alpha}$ $\tau\acute{\alpha}\varphi\rho o\nu$ $\grave{o}\varrho\acute{\nu}x\overline{\imath}\eta\nu$. Homer.

† 'Aπò τῆς Θαλάσσης, ὡς ἐπὶ τὴν εὠ, ὡς εἰς μεσογαῖαν τῆς
Εὐρώπης. Polyb.

As

As I mention the army marching in two columns, it may alſo be expected, that I explain whence I took that opinion. I did ſuppoſe, that the detachment commanded by Hanno did continue to act as a detached corps ; and, for a ſimilar reaſon as that why it paſſed at a different traject, it would march on the left flank of the main body, to cover it from any defulrory irruptions upon its line of march from the enemy. The uſe of that diſpoſition would ceaſe when the army arrived at Ambrone, where other diſpoſitions muſt be made. Now, ſurely, I would hope, that without any imputation of confuſedneſs, I may ſuppoſe, that when it entered the defiles of the Alps, it might have marched in one column over one and the ſame ridge, whichſoever that might be. The reader will obſerve, that I did not venture to ſuppoſe, much leſs preſume *to aſcertain*, which that was.

Well, but as my eye went to Ambrone, Mr. Whitaker will make my opinion go over the Mont Genevre ; and, as I mentioned the White Rock, he will make me go alſo over the Little St. Bernard,

over

over two very different and diftant paffes, in one and the fame rout.

I might have followed up my ideas one ftage farther, to Mont Dauphin; and yet, when there, it was not neceffary I fhould go to Mount Genevre. I might have fup-pofed another rout; as at Mount Dau-phin the road divides, going in one direc-tion over Mount Genevre, in another up the vale of Quieras, and thence down the vale of Lucerna to the Po. As to the white rock, I mention that in a paren thefis, as a diftinctive mark to be ob-ferved, wherefoever Hannibal's courfe fhould be fuppofed to pafs. I did not, nor could I be fuppofed to mean or to refer * to the white rock faid to be dif-covered by General Melville, in his rout over the Little St. Bernard; I had not at that time, nor have I fince, feen his Me-moire on that fubject. Mr. Whitaker might as well fuppofe me to mean and to refer to *his white rock*, which he finds in his courfe over the Grand St. Bernard:

---

* I have within thefe few days been fhewn a map, whereon General Melville has, by a red line, traced his idea of Hannibal's courfe. Bath, June 9, 1794.

for,

for indeed, as he fays *, " a white-rock
" would not be difficult to be found
" upon † any of the lines drawn for Han-
" nibal's movements."

If, therefore, it had been my purpofe,
or I had thought it worth my while, to
follow with my opinion the trace of Hannibal's march beyond Ambrone ‡, " I
" would not, in the eafy acquiefcence of
" a lazy antiquarianifm, have contented
" myfelf with the mere cafuality of a
" white rock occurring. I would have
" examined the particular pofition of the
" rock, and marked how accommodable
" it were to the tenor of the hiftory."

I fhall not now, as I did not, when I
curforily mentioned *the fuppofed march* of
Hannibal from Beaucaire to Ambrone,
enter into any difquifition of the general
fubject. My only aim in thefe remarks
is to exculpate *my notices* from the charge
of inaccuracy and ignorance imputed to

* Whitaker, vol. I. p. 269.
† Why then will Mr. Whitaker make it *neceffary*, that
my opinion fhould lead over Little St. Bernard for the fake
of a white rock which is faid to lie in that rout, when a
white rock, he fays, may be found in any ?
‡ Whitaker, vol. I. p. 270.

P   them

them by the Rev. Mr. Whitaker in two
or three parts."

I was not ignorant that there were three
opinions as to the courſe of Hannibal's
march. Paſſing down from the heights
of Montlimart, the ſight of the great
plain below, which I deſcribe *, as the
Delta of Gaul, brought to my mind the
the † opinion which I had adopted, as
the *probable* one ; and I amuſed myſelf
with tracing by my eye this *ſuppoſed
courſe* of Hannibal's march. - I am very
little ſolicitous whether this be thought
to be the right one. If Mr. Whitaker
ſhall think it is not, I ſhall leave the
point, which of the other two be the
right one, to be ſettled by General Melville and Mr. Whitaker, by the one who,
as a ſcholar, and an officer, maſter of
his profeſſion, examined the *local* with
his own eyes : and compared it with the
hiſtory on the ſpot ; and by the other,

---

* I am not ignorant, that the iſland deſcribed by Polybius and Livy, has been called *the Delta* ; yet, without
controverting that opinion, as the tract of land which I
deſcribe *at the Delta* is more ſimilar in circumſtances and
form to the Delta of Egypt, transferred that name to it,
and call it the *Delta of Gaul.*

† This opinion has alſo been adopted in the great map
of the Italian dominions of the King of Sardinia, made
under the authority of Government.

who,

who, as an ingenious critic, and learned author, " *afcertains it by the glaffes of* " *hiftory*" in his clofet. I fhall leave it to thefe gentlemen to fettle whether Hanni-bal in his march went up the vale of the Ifar by Grenoble, and thence over the Little St. Bernard; or whether he marched all the way up the vale of the Rhone to Lyons, and thence over the Grand St. Bernard. There are fome probabilities, and many difficulties to be met with in both thefe opinions.

If I were difpofed to give up the opinion I had adopted, and were farther inclined to interpofe any opinion as to thefe two other routs, I could go with fuch my opi-nion in company with thefe gentlemen as far as *the ifland**, that infulated tract of country furrounded by the Rhone and the Ifar, which was the principal habitation of the Allobroges, named *the ifland* from its being fo bounded.

---

* Quartis caftris, ad *Infulam* pervevit. Ubi Arar Rhodonufque amnes diverfis ex Alpibus decurrentes, agri aliquantum amplexi, confluunt in unum. Mediis campis Infulæ nomen inditum incolant *prope* Allobroges.—Note Crevieri—non *prope* ut Livius, fed in ipfa infula incollere Allobroges dicit Polybius.

Poly-

Polybius feems to fay (Lib. 9, § 47.) that Hannibal paffed the Alps by the fources of the Rhone: but if the printed editions do actually contain Polybius's precife opinion; yet the rout by which he went is not afcertained. Both Polybius and Livy fay, indeed, (according to the printed editions,) that he went up to point, or fork, where the Rhone and *Arar* unite, and defcribe the tract between thefe two rivers as an ifland. But the river, here called the Arar, is defcribed as coming from the Alps as well as the Rhone. Now the Arar rifing in Franche Comte, running through Burgundy, and joining the Rhone at Lyons, never comes within ninety miles of the Alps; whereas the Ifar rifes in, and comes from, the Alps. Nor do the Arar and Rhone furround any tract of country in a manner fo as it may be called an ifland; whereas the Rhone and Ifar actually do, the tract between their courfes being almoft *, within a fmall fpace of being entirely, furrounded by them. Nor, laftly, did the Allobroges dwell between the Rhone and the *Arar*, but between the Rhone and the *Ifar*.

* At, Les Echelles.

I could

I could not, therefore, accompany with
my opinion Mr. Whitaker higher up the
Rhone, nor go with him to Lyons. My
opinion would lead me with General
Melville acrofs this ifland about twenty
pofts E N E, in the direction of the Ifar.
I think Mr. Whitaker might accompany
us fo far; and yet not give up his pafs
by the fources of the Rhone over the
Grand St. Bernard. For if he would,
inftead of reprobating Livy * *for turning
to the left*, he might turn thence, and go
with him to the left to Chamberry:
whilft General Melville goes off upon the
right to Grenoble, and keeps up the vale
of the Ifar. Mr. Whitaker might thence,
having paffed through the country of his
friends the Allobroges, the Tricaftines,
&c. come again upon the Rhone, by a
better and fhorter way. This gentleman,
however, abiding by the printed letter,
rather than looking to the geography, the
topography, and inhabitancy of the country, takes the point of land between the
Rhone and the Arar to be this ifland.
Upon a more critical re-examination of

---

* Sedatis certaminibus Allobragum, quum jam Alpes
peteret, non recta regione iter inftituit fed ad lævam in
Tricaftinos flexit. Inde, &c. Livius, lib. 21, § 31.

P 3   this

this point, I am convinced that this gentleman is miftaken, and concludes not
only without, but againft, evidence.

I have faid thus much upon a fuppofi-,
tion that I was difpofed to give up the
opinion which I had adopted, and with
which I amufed myfelf; but as I am
not, as yet, fo difpofed, I will, if Mr.
Whitaker will be fo kind as not to infift
upon my adopting any opinion farther
than I did adopt it, and will permit me
to ftop at Ambrone, I will remain ftationary there ; refting on conjecture, until
he and General Melville fhall have fettled which of the two routs is the right
one, *afcertained* as a matter of fact.

NUMBER III.

Mr. Whitaker, in a third note, (vol. I.
p. 136.) makes a criticifm on my calling
the Allobroges *Allaboroughs*, or *Ailb'roughs*.
He fays the word is neceffarily *Celtic* ;
and ftates me as a writer who knows not
Britifh. I will not enter into any difcuf-
fion about the Celtic language, nor into
any

2

any queſtion how far the Cymric or Britiſh was ſpecifically Celtic. It is poſſible
I may have (no offence I hope) as juſt a
notion of this as himſelf, even though I
knew nothing of Britiſh.

I will, however, venture to ſuggeſt to
his greater learning and more enlarged
information a query, whether Brog, or
Brox, as it is enounced by the Romans,
may not be a traduċtive term from Bourg,
a word of the Teutiſch, or old Deutſch
language, remaining even at this day
common in Germany. This word, although in the courſe of time it was applied to exprefs a town or city, was uſed
originally as a name to exprefs the Pagus
or Civitas (not Urbs) at large. There are
ſeveral towns called ſimply Bourg, and
more with the termination bourg affixed
to ſome ſpecifick name, as Straas-bourg,
Magde-bourg, Lunen-bourg, Branden-
bourg, &c.

Although Mr. Whitaker, rather con-
temptuouſly, ſuppoſes me to be ignorant
of every other language, and for that reaſon to make the word an Engliſh one
ſcil. borough or b'rough; yet, I will
venture to ſay, that Engliſh word is only

traduc-

traductive from the old Deutfch word brog, or b'rog.

That Englifh terms have been thus traductive even from the Greek language, I prefent him with one inftance. The term, generally ufed as a termination affixed, *Bury*, or Bery, is derived from the term Βρια; alfo ufed in the fame manner in feveral inftances, fignifying Πολις.

But, perhaps, this learned critic may think *his Celtic word Brog*, means breeches; and that thefe Allobroges were called from a peculiarity in their cloathing *Allbreeches*, Galli braccati; as the name of a Dutch family, which I knew, was *Tenbrog*', from Ten-breeches. If he does, I will not controvert the point with him.

But I have unfortunately faid that the Allobroges, or Allb'roughs, were a republick; and, in confequence of this, have incurred from the Rev. Mr. Whitaker this inquifitorial cenfure, as follows: " This frenzy of freedom, this igno-" rance of language, have fure rifen to " their *higheft noon* together, when a

4

" name,

" name, importing only the nation to
" be Gaul, is made to prove them a
" *Republick*, and a Republick of bo-
" roughs."

My Notices were written and publifhed many years before the word *Repub-*
lick, in confequence of the abufe and per-
verfion of it, was made a party term, de-
noting a fpirit of faction in thofe who
ufed it. But I plead not to an inquifition refpecting my political principles;
I will appeal from it to the cool delibe-
rate judgement and integrity of Mr.
Whitaker : and, affured of not rifquing
any ungentlemanlike imputation from
this gentleman, I will venture to repeat
that the government of the Allobroges
was a Republick, a Fœderation of B'roughs;
each borough adminiftered by their Principes, and the whole in its civil government by the Principes and Senate *Senatus*
Principumque Sententiâ *. The power of
the principes was merely authoritative,
not coercive, *authoritate fuadendi magis,*
quam jubendi poteftate †. The military
command of this Republick was an *im-*

---

* Livius, lib. 21, § 31.

† Tacitus de Mor. Germ. § 11.

perium

perium, executed by an *Imperator*, who was elective, chosen by the Principes and Senate.

If Mr. Whitaker consults Cæsar's Commentaries (Lib. 7, § 64,), if he consults Cicero (Orat. 3 in Catilinam,), or Salluft, for an account of the Ambaffadors of the Allobroges, he will find they were delegates, not of any King, or other perfon having monarchical power, but of the people *Allobrogum* : and he will find, farther, that when any negotiation was to be carried on with thefe people, it was not entered into with a King, but with the Principes *, as preparatory to a settlement with a nation at large.

If Mr. Whitaker wifhes to be more particularly informed of the fpecies of republican government which I refer to, I will refer him to Tacitus de Moribus

---

* Nihilo minus clandeftinis nunciis, legationibufque Allobroges follicitat ; quorum nientes nondum à fuperiore bello refidiffe fperabat. Horum Principibus pecunias, Civitati autem imperium totius provinciæ pollicetur. De Bell. Gall. l. 7. § 64.

Catiline employed Umbro to treat with the Allobroges, P. Umbreno cuidam negotium dat—qued in Gallia negotiatus erat, plerifque Principibus Civitatum notus erat atque eos noverat. Salluft Bell. Catil.

Ger-

Germanorum, where he will find defcribed a government of the fame fort.

NUMBER IV.

Mr. Whitaker roundly and pofitively
afferts, that the four columns, mentioned
by me in my *Notices*, which fupport the
dome of a church at Lyons, " are beau-
" tiful columns of Egyptian granite."
I had faid " that they are of granite, not
" Egyptian, but of a fpecies which are
" found in the mountains of Dauphiné."
When I faid this, I faid it from the information and on the authority of Acade-
micians, great naturalifts, living on the
fpot. And when I fay, " that it is ap-
" parent that they have been made out
" of two fawn afunder, and that they
" are now four misfhapen difproportion-
" ed fupports called columns," I venture to fay this from my own view, and
my own knowledge of what the form
and proportion of a column ought to be.
I will not here retort on this gentleman
by a fimilar mode of direct contradiction,

fuch

such as he ufes. I will only beg that
Mr. Whitaker would either himfelf examine this fact on the fpot, or get fome
naturalift to examine the *matter* of them,
and fome architect to examine the *form*,
before he decides fo peremptorily. If he
does, I will venture to fay, he will coin-
cide with, not contradict, my affertion
and opinion.

CLOSE.

CLOSE.

I will here, with my refpects to Mr. Whitaker's literary abilities, clofe thefe papers. I will beg that Mr. Whitaker will not confider me, as entering into controverfy with him about thefe learned trifles. I have neither leifure nor inclination to employ my time in fuch matters, at a period of my life, when things of higher import and more ferious concern ought to engage my attention. If what I have written here does not fatisfy him; let him reft fatisfied in himfelf, that I am wrong, and he is right. He may enjoy the idea of a literary victory over me; I fhall not conteft it; he may erect his trophies on the field of battle; and, if he can obtain from the *Republick* of Letters, and will accept from a Republick the honour of a triumph, he may erect a triumphal arch on any favourite fpot of Hannibal's courfe *afcertained*; or in the *kingdom* of the Allobroges.

F I N I S.

NEW BOOKS LATELY PUBLISHED BY JOHN NICHOLS.

I. Twelve Prints of Monafteries, Caftles, antient Churches, and Monuments, in the County of Suffolk, drawn by Jofhua Kirby, Pain-
ter, in Ipfwich, and publifhed by him in
1748. Price 16s.
₊ Very few Copies remain ; and the Plates, it is
believed, are deftroyed.

II. Four new Numbers of Mifcellaneous
Antiquities (in continuation of the Bibliotheca
Topographica Britannica); namely,

. 1. *Manduefſedum Romanorum*; being the Hiftory and Antiquities of the Parifh of Man-
ceter [including the Hamlets of Hartfhill, Old-
bury, and Atherftone], and alfo of the adja-
cent Parifh of Anfley, in the County of War-
wick. By the late Mr. Benjamin Bartlett, F.S.A.
enlarged and correfted under the Infpeftion of
feveral Gentlemen refident upon the Spot. Price
10s. 6d.

. 2. A Sketch of the Hiftory and Antiquities of Hawkherft ; upon the Plan fuggefted
in the Gentleman's Magazine, for procuring
Parochial Hiftories throughout England.
Price 2s.

3. The Hiftory of the Manor and Manor-
Houfe of South Winfield, in Derbyfhire.
By Thomas Blore, of the Society of the
Middle Temple, and F.S.A. Price 10s. 6d.

4. The Hiftory and Antiquities of Shen-
fton, in the County of Stafford ; together
with the Pedigrees of all the Families, both
antient

antient and modern, of that Parifh. By the late Rev. H. Sanders, of Oriel College, Oxford, many Years Curate of that Parifh. With a View of the Church ; and fome Account of the Author. Price 12s.

III. Annales Eliæ de Trickingham, Monachi Ordinis Benedictini. Ex Bibliothecâ Lamethanâ. Epiftola ad Johannem Nicholfium, celeberrimum Typographum, præmittitur. In quâ de Auctore et ejus Opere fufè agitur; et neceffariæ infuper Adnotatiunculæ adjunguntur. Subnectitur Compendium Compertorium, per Tho. Legh et Ric. Layton, Vifitatores Regios ; ex Bibliothecâ Ducis Devoniæ. Unà cum Anteloquio de Naturâ Operis, et Vitas Vifitatorum complectente. Notulæ hinc inde infperfæ funt. Utrumque Opufculum ex MSS. nunc primum edidit Samuel Pegge, A.M. 4to, Price 5s.

IV. The Life of Robert Groffetefte, the celebrated Bifhop of Lincoln, by Samuel Pegge, LL.D. Prebendary of Lowth in that Church ; with an Account of the Bifhop's Works, and an Appendix. 4to. Price 13s. in Boards.

V. A Tour through the Ifle of Thanet, and fome other Parts of Eaft Kent ; including a particular Defcription of the Churches in that extenfive Diftrict ; and Copies of the Monumental Infcriptions, &c. 4to. Price 16s.

VI. The Monuments and Painted Glafs of upwards of One Hundred Churches, chiefly in the Eaftern Part of Kent ; moft

of

of which were examined by the Editor in
Perfon, and the reft communicated by the
Refident Clergy. With an Appendix, con-
taining Three Churches in other Counties.
To which are added a fmall Collection of detached Epitaphs, with a few Notes on the
whole. By Philip Parfons, M. A. Minifter
of Wye in Kent. 4to. Price 18s.

VII. The Will of King Henry the Eighth,
from an authentic Copy in the Hands of an
Attorney, with an Introductory Preface, con-
taining fome Obfervations on the Conduct of
that Monarch, with a View to induce the
Reader's Reflexions on, and forming a Com-
parifon of, the Difference between that King's
Character and Actions, and thofe of our prefent gracious Sovereign. 4to, Price 2s. 6d.

VIII. *Notitia Monaftica* ; or, an Account
of all the Abbeys, Priories, and Houfes
of Friers, formerly in England and Wales.
And alfo of all the Colleges and Hofpitals
founded before A. D. 1540. By the Right
Reverend Dr. Thomas Tanner, Lord Bifhop of
St. Afaph. Publifhed, A. D. 1744, by John
Tanner, M. A. Vicar of Loweftoft in Suffolk,
and Precentor of the Cathedral Church of St.
Afaph. And now re-printed, with many Ad-
ditions, by James Nafmith, M. A. Rector of
Snalewell, Cambridgefhire, and Chaplain to
the Earl of Buckinghamfhire. Folio. Price
Two Guineas in Boards.